CUB IN THE CUPBOARD

Lucy Daniels

Illustrated by Shelagh McNicholas

First published in Great Britain 1994 by
Hodder Children's Books
This Large Print edition published by
BBC Audiobooks Ltd
by arrangement with
Hodder & Stoughton Ltd 2005

ISBN 1 4056 6049 X

Text copyright © 1998 Working Partners
Limited
Created by Working Partners Limited,
London W6 0QT
Original series created by Ben M. Baglio
Illustrations © Shelagh McNicholas 1994

British Library Cataloguing in Publication Data available

Printed and bound in Great Britain by
Antony Rowe Ltd., Chippenham, Wiltshire

Special thanks to Helen Magee.
Thanks also to C. J. Hall, B.Vet.Med.,
M.R.C.V.S. for reviewing the veterinary
information contained in this book.

CHAPTER ONE

The sound of bells floated on the air as Mandy Hope and her friend, James Hunter, crested the hill above Welford. They halted their bikes and looked down on the scene below. Welford lay spread out before them like a toy village.

'Look, there's Mr Hardy coming out of the Fox and Goose,' said Mandy pointing to the pub where the village's two streets crossed.

'And there's Animal Ark,' said James.

Animal Ark was Mandy's home. It was also her mum and dad's veterinary practice. 'Look, Simon is just arriving,'

James went on.

Mandy looked down on the old, stone cottage with the modern extension at the back. A fair-haired, young man was just turning the corner of the house. Simon was the practice nurse at Animal Ark.

The bells rang out even louder and she switched her attention to the church. 'Gran and Grandad should be back soon,' she said to James. Mandy's grandparents were on a tour of the Border country of the north of England.

'Back from the wilds of Northumberland,' James said, smiling. 'They're real travellers, your gran and grandad, ever since they got that camper van.'

Mandy laughed. 'Gran certainly is,' she said. 'We got a postcard from her. They've been doing a lot of hill walking. But sometimes I think Grandad would be happier staying in Welford with his vegetables and his bell-ringing.'

Another peal from the church tower startled the rooks nesting in the trees around the church. They rose into the air in a great cloud of black, beating wings.

'Walter Pickard seems to be doing all right with those bells without any help,' said James.

Mandy laughed again. 'Grandad says he gets carried away sometimes.' She lifted her head and let the fresh spring breeze cool her cheeks. They were hot from the effort of cycling to the top of the hill.

'Race you to the bottom of the hill,' James said.

Mandy swung her head round, short, fair hair blowing across her eyes. She shook it back and grinned at James. He shoved his glasses more securely up on to his nose and grinned back at her.

'Where's the finishing line?' she said.

James looked thoughtful. 'The bridge over the stream at the bottom of the hill,' he said. 'By Monkton Spinney.'

'OK,' said Mandy. 'You're on!' And she set off, flying down the hill, free-wheeling as the steepness of the slope increased.

'Wait for me!' James shouted, but she hardly heard him.

The wind flattened Mandy's jumper against her chest and her hair fluttered free of her face. Above her the sky was blue, around her the countryside was fresh and green. It was one of those magical spring days when all was right with the world.

They were neck and neck as they approached the bridge where the road narrowed. Mandy put on an extra spurt and drew just ahead of James as they reached the bridge.

'I won, I won!' she cried as she slowed her bike to a halt at the other end of the bridge.

James swerved and came to a sliding halt beside her. 'Only just,' he said.

They stood there for a moment astride their bikes, catching their breath. The air was still and warm down in the shelter of the valley. They could hear small sounds. The call of a bird in the wood, the rustle of some small creature in the undergrowth and a fish splashing as it surfaced right below the bridge.

4

Here, the water was smooth and free running but further along, as it flowed through the wood, it became rougher. Mandy gazed at the water. Then she started.

'What was that?' she said.

James turned to her as she swung her bike round. 'What?' he said slewing his own bike round and stopping just in front of her.

Mandy frowned. 'I heard something,' she said. 'Down there.' She pointed down towards the little wood on their right.

James looked where she was pointing. 'In Monkton Spinney?' he said. Then he looked at her face. 'What kind of noise?'

Mandy shook her head and pushed the hair out of her eyes. 'I don't know,' she said. 'It sounded like a cry.'

'Like a baby?' said James. He was clearly puzzled.

Mandy looked down towards the spinney. Through the trees, she could see the rush of water as the stream tumbled through the rocks which edged the steep banks. The water

5

gleamed silver in the sunlight. Then the sound came again; a thin cry swept away on the breeze.

'There,' said Mandy. 'There it is again.'

James bit his lip. 'It doesn't sound like a baby to me,' he said. 'More like an animal.'

'Yes,' said Mandy. 'It is an animal. It's an animal in trouble.' She swung one long leg over her bike and stood beside it, her face intent. 'We've got to find it, James. We've got to help it.'

James looked at her. There was no arguing with Mandy when she thought there was an animal in trouble. Not that James wanted to argue. He loved animals nearly as much as Mandy did. 'What about your mum?' he said. 'We promised her we'd meet her at The Riddings at two. It's nearly that now.'

Mandy bit her lip. She and James had been on their way to see Patch, a kitten the Spry sisters had adopted from them a while ago. Mrs Hope had said she would meet them there. The Sprys were elderly ladies and they didn't like coming into Animal Ark

6

with Patch. But Mrs Hope didn't mind making calls. Patch meant so much to the sisters. Having him had really changed their lives. Before they adopted the kitten they had been real hermits. Now they were beginning to come out of their shells.

'We might miss her,' said James. 'And then you wouldn't get to see Patch. The Sprys let hardly anybody into that big house of theirs.'

Mandy frowned. It was true. And she hadn't seen Patch since the sisters took him in. But that cry had sounded serious. She made up her mind.

'It can't be helped,' she said. 'Mum will understand. After all she's a vet. She'd do the same if she thought she could help an animal in trouble.'

Just then another cry floated up from the wood—more piercing this time, a cry of real pain. Mandy strained her eyes to see into the wood but the shadows were dark beneath the trees. It was hard to see. She turned back to James but he was already off his bike and wheeling it to the side of the road.

'That sounded bad,' he said. 'What

do you think it is?'

Mandy shook her head as she wheeled her bike off the bridge and leaned it against the low dry-stone wall that bordered the road. 'I don't know,' she said. 'It sounds a bit like a dog in pain.'

James frowned, 'Well, if anything happened to Blackie I'd want somebody to investigate it,' he said. Blackie was James's Labrador.

Mandy nodded. 'Then let's go!' she said.

She was off, long legs leaping the wall, feet flying as she sped through the bracken towards the little wood.

'Hey, wait for me!' said James but Mandy didn't hear. Hair flying, feet leaping the tussocks of grass, she covered the distance between the road and the wood in long, easy strides. When it came to an animal in trouble there was only one thing on Mandy's mind—helping.

She reached the wood out of breath with James crashing behind her. 'Shh,' she said. 'We don't want to frighten it. Where do you think it is?'

8

James looked round. The little wood was quiet except for the sound of their breathing and the splash of water on rocks. A blackbird trilled but there was no other sound—no sound to guide them to where an animal was in pain. Then, sharp and clear it came again—a long drawn out cry echoing into the stillness of the wood. It died away as if whatever made it was growing weaker.

Mandy turned swiftly to her right. 'Over there,' she said, pointing down towards a deep depression in the ground where the wood sloped away towards the rocks. James made to run but Mandy stopped him. 'We'll have to be very quiet,' she said. 'A hurt animal can do itself even more harm if it's frightened.'

Slowly, carefully, they crept down through the wood towards the hollow. There were ferns growing all down the sides of the slope, covering anything that might be down there. The cry came once more and Mandy parted a clump of ferns and looked into the hollow. At first she couldn't see anything. Then she saw a movement, a

9

reddish-brown something stirring the ferns at the bottom of the hollow.

'Down there,' she said.

As quietly as they could, they made their way down the slope until they came to the place where the sound had come from. Gently, Mandy parted the ferns. For a moment she stood, unable to move.

'What is it?' said James from behind.

Mandy turned a white face to him and just shook her head. She didn't seem able to speak.

James came to stand beside her. At their feet, not a metre away, lay a fox, its eyes glazed with pain and fear. Its leg was caught in a steel trap, the blood dried and matted now.

As they stood there the fox lifted its head slightly and looked at them. Its eyes flickered in terror and again it gave the cry they had heard, but weaker now. It tried to squirm free of the trap to get away from them and there was another fresh spurt of blood from its wound.

Mandy could feel its terror. She reached out a hand and laid it on the

10

fox's side. Its fur was the colour of autumn leaves. 'Don't,' she said. 'Don't struggle. You'll only make it worse.'

The sound of her voice, gentle and soothing, seemed to calm the terrified animal. 'We'll get you out,' Mandy was saying when James took her elbow.

'Look, Mandy,' he said. 'Look!' His voice sounded funny.

Mandy looked where he was pointing. Huddled beneath the fox where the ferns hid them from sight were four newborn cubs, their fur glistening, their eyes tightly closed. Their fur was dark and woolly, and they looked more like Alsatian puppies than foxes.

Mandy gasped. 'They can't be more than an hour old,' she said.

James nodded and gulped as Mandy bent to the cubs. When she didn't say anything more he said, 'What's the matter?'

Mandy lifted her face to his. Tears were streaming down it. 'They're dead, James,' she said. 'The cubs are dead. The vixen must have given birth early and now her cubs are dead.'

James swallowed hard. 'At least we can try to save her,' he said. 'Come on, Mandy.'

He was down on his knees beside the trap, trying to force the cruel steel jaws apart. In a second Mandy was beside him, her face still stained with tears but hope in her voice. 'The trap hasn't closed completely. Look, there's a stone wedged in it—here between the teeth.' James looked. The trap had sprung nearly together but a stone had been caught in it, wedging it slightly open.

'If we can just move the vixen's leg a couple of centimetres we can get it through the gap,' Mandy said.

'Be careful,' said James. 'If you dislodge that stone the trap will spring tighter.'

Mandy looked at the steel jaws of the trap with their sharp, jagged edges. She shivered. One wrong move and the thing would spring really tightly shut and the vixen's leg would be shattered.

They worked very gently, easing the vixen's leg millimetre by millimetre until they got it in position.

'Now!' said Mandy and together they lifted the leg clear of the teeth of the trap. The vixen yelped and tried to snarl at them but she was too weak to do anything. Her deep brown eyes were full of pain. The leg came free and Mandy heaved a sigh of relief.

Feeling her freedom, the vixen tried to stand and, as she did so, she nudged the trap. The stone fell and the trap's jaws sprang together like a vice. The sound made Mandy jump with fright. She stared at the trap in horror. Mandy had always hated such things, but it wasn't until that moment that she fully realised just how cruel they were.

'What have you done to your hand?' James said. Mandy looked down. There was blood on her hand.

'Oh,' she said. 'That must have happened when the trap sprang closed.'

James looked worried. 'You'd better put something round it to stop the blood,' he said.

Mandy pulled out a handkerchief and wiped her hand with it. 'It's nothing,' she said. 'It's just a graze.'

'Does it hurt?' said James.

Mandy turned to him. 'As if that matters. We did it, James. We got the vixen out of the trap!'

James looked down. 'She looks pretty weak,' he said. 'What are we going to do?'

There was no answer.

'Mandy?' he said.

But Mandy was staring at the vixen as she edged nearer to her poor dead cubs, dragging her wounded leg behind her. They watched as she nuzzled and nudged at the cubs, licking one and then another. Then she seemed to concentrate on one cub, nudging, licking, nuzzling. Mandy felt the prick of tears. 'Poor thing,' she said. 'Doesn't she know they're dead?'

Then incredibly, as they watched, there was a movement. The cub the vixen was concentrating on stirred and moved and tried to nuzzle blindly towards its mother. The vixen nudged it into position and it began to feed.

Mandy looked at the vixen. She was weak with loss of blood and the effort of dragging herself to her little cub. But instinct had triumphed over hurt and pain. She had thought of her cubs first. Her eyes were closed now but the cub was feeding, its black furry sides heaving.

Mandy turned a shining face on James. 'One of the cubs is alive,' she said. 'Alive, James!'

James pursed his lips. 'What about the vixen though?' he said. 'She looks pretty weak.'

Mandy bit her lip. 'We can't just leave them here,' she said. 'They would never survive. James, you've got to go to the Sprys and get Mum. Tell her to come as quickly as she can. I'll stay here and keep watch in case . . .'

'In case what?' said James.

Mandy's face set. 'Nothing,' she said. 'Just go, James—and hurry.'

She watched him go, her mouth still set in a grim line. She wasn't going to leave mother and child—not when they still had a chance to survive. And she had to stay—in case whoever had set the trap came back and finished off their dirty work. Mandy sat there, stroking the vixen's deep red coat. She watched the cub struggling for life and wondered who could have been so cruel.

CHAPTER TWO

It was the longest half-hour of Mandy's life. She sat watching over the vixen and her cub until the little animal finished feeding and crept even closer to his mother's side.

Mandy looked at the vixen. Her eyes were still closed. Mandy's breath stopped in her throat. She could see no sign of life.

Gently she put a hand to the vixen's side. She was still breathing. Mandy could feel the slight rise and fall of her side. But she was getting cold despite her thick coat.

Mandy looked around desperately for something to cover the two animals with—something to keep them warm.

17

There was nothing. Quickly she pulled off her jumper and tucked it round vixen and cub, stroking the vixen's head and murmuring to her.

'It won't be long now,' she said. James will be back soon with Mum and then everything will be fine. You'll see. Mum and Dad look after lots of animals at Animal Ark.'

The vixen's dark eyes opened briefly as Mandy spoke. It was as if they were pleading with her for help. Mandy laid a hand on the vixen's pointed muzzle and continued to speak in a soothing, comforting voice. She knew that talking gently to hurt animals helped to calm them. It helped to keep their pulses steady and to reassure them if they were in shock. So she sat by the vixen and her cub and told them all about Welford and Animal Ark and her mother and father, Adam and Emily Hope, who were vets, and Gran and Grandad who lived in the village and James, her best friend, and his Labrador, Blackie.

She was deep in a description of Gran and Grandad's new camper van when she felt the cub squirm under her jumper and make a tiny sound. Mandy smiled in spite of her worry. 'You're a fighter, aren't you?' she said.

Just then there was a sound of a car engine and the scrape of tyres drawing up. *Mum and James*, Mandy thought, then she hesitated. It could be the person who had set the trap! If it was, she would have to be careful. She bit her lip as she looked down at the two helpless animals. Even if it was the trap setter, the animals would still be safe. Mandy would see to that.

She leaped to her feet and scrambled up the banking. There was a sound of voices and a bright flash of red hair beyond the trees. There was no mistaking Mrs Hope's hair. It glowed like copper. It was Mum and James after all.

'Mum!' she called. 'Over here. Hurry!'

Mrs Hope and James came running through the trees. Mandy thought she had never been so glad to see her mum.

'I was as quick as possible,' said

James.

Mandy smiled. 'I know. It just seemed like an age, that's all.'

'Well,' said Mrs Hope, smiling down at Mandy. 'I hear you've rescued a fox this time.' Her green eyes were bright with concern. Looking at them, Mandy felt a terrific sense of relief. It would be all right now that Mum was here.

'And a cub, Mum,' said Mandy, almost pushing her mother down towards the hollow in her eagerness. 'But the vixen is hurt and very weak and the cub is so tiny. You can help them, Mum, can't you?'

Emily Hope looked down at the anxious faces of James and Mandy. 'I can do my best,' she said gently. Then her voice became brisk. 'Now, where are my patients?'

Mandy pointed to her green jumper tucked round the foxes. 'There,' she said and Mrs Hope smiled.

'Is that the new one Gran knitted for you?' she said.

'Gran won't mind,' said Mandy. 'It's in a good cause.'

She felt so much better now that her

20

mum was here with her vet's bag and her gentle hands, kneeling beside the foxes, undoing Mandy's jumper, searching with quick, practised fingers for injury.

Mrs Hope understood how Mandy felt about animals, especially young orphaned animals. She understood because she and Adam Hope had adopted Mandy when Mandy became an orphan. Mandy's real parents had been killed in a car crash when she was a baby but, for her, Adam and Emily Hope were as real as any mum and dad could be. In fact to Mandy they were the best mum and dad in the world.

At last Emily Hope straightened up. Her face was serious and Mandy's heart sank.

'You *can* help, can't you, Mrs Hope?' James said.

Mandy's mum pursed her lips. 'The vixen has lost a lot of blood,' she said. 'She's very weak. The wound in her upper leg is deep. If we move her it might start to bleed again.'

Mandy nodded. 'It *did* start to bleed again when she tried to move.'

Emily Hope nodded. It isn't just that, Mandy. It's also the blood she has lost after giving birth. I'm afraid the shock of being caught in the trap brought it on early. Animals in shock are much less likely to survive, you know.'

'Can't you do anything, Mum?' Mandy said.

Emily Hope shook her head. 'Not here,' she said. 'I need clean water for a start.' She looked around the wood. The light filtered dimly through the trees. 'And I need a good light to work in. I'll have to stitch this leg and I think there's a good chance she'll need an operation.'

Then we'll take them to Animal Ark,' Mandy said.

Mrs Hope didn't say anything for a moment.

'Mum?' said Mandy. 'What's wrong?'

Mrs Hope sighed. 'Mandy,' she said slowly, 'if I move her it might be too much for her. Animal Ark is too far away. I don't think I'd get her there alive.'

Mandy was close to tears. 'What about the cub?' she said. 'Can you save the cub?'

Emily Hope's eyes were sad. 'I'm afraid the cub can't survive without his mother—not for two or three weeks yet.'

'But we have to do something,' said James. 'We can't just leave them to die.'

Mrs Hope nodded. 'I agree,' she said. 'We'll try to get them to Animal Ark. I just wanted you to understand the risks.'

'No,' said Mandy suddenly. 'It's too dangerous.' James and Mrs Hope looked at her.

'You mean you want to leave them here?' said James as if he couldn't believe his ears.

Mandy shook her head. 'No,' she said. 'I want to take them to The Riddings. It's only five minutes away by car. Could you manage to work there, Mum? Would that do?'

Emily Hope looked doubtful, then she said. 'Yes, I could manage. It's certainly better than trying to take the animals all the way to Animal Ark.'

'What will the Spry sisters say?' said James.

Mandy shrugged. 'We'll see when we get there,' she said. 'Come on, James. There's no time to lose.'

'There's a sack in the back of the car, Mandy,' Emily Hope said. 'Run and fetch it. We can use it as a stretcher.'

When Mandy got back with the sack she found that her mum had put a tight bandage round the vixen's leg.

'This will stop it bleeding,' said Emily Hope. 'But there's no time to waste. We can't leave that on too long or the leg will be permanently damaged. You can only stop the blood getting to it for so long without risk.'

Mandy spread the sack out and Mrs Hope laid the vixen on top. 'You take one end and I'll take the other, James,' she said. 'And be careful. The vixen is too weak to snap just at the moment. But don't forget, she's a wild animal. Mandy, you can bring the cub.'

Mandy picked up the scrap of life that was the cub. He was so tiny. But he was warm and his little tongue flicked out and rubbed against her hand as she held him. Then she looked down and felt her throat tighten.

'Mum,' she said. 'What about the other cubs, the ones that didn't survive? We can't just leave them here like this.'

Mrs Hope stretched out a hand and laid it on Mandy's shoulder. 'We have to—for the moment,' she said. 'We have to try to save the vixen and her cub. It's a hard lesson to learn, Mandy, but the living come first.'

Mandy felt tears prick behind her eyes. But her mum was right. Even the vixen had wasted no time on the cubs that she couldn't help. Instead she had saved the one who was still alive. It was the instinct of survival.

'Dad will come up later and bury these little ones,' Emily Hope said.

Mandy nodded. She couldn't speak. But she knew that what her mother said made sense even if it was hard to accept.

The little procession made its way up out of the hollow towards the road where Mrs Hope's four-wheel drive waited. James took the back seat with the vixen beside him and Mandy slid into the seat beside her mother, the tiny cub cradled in her arms.

She looked down at the little bundle of fur. At least this one had a chance of surviving—if they could save its mother. 'Oh, please let us be in time,' she whispered. 'Please.'

*   *   *

The Riddings was a huge old house set back from wide sweeping lawns. As Mrs Hope drove up the driveway towards the massive stone staircase in front of the house Mandy looked at the turrets and battlements. What a place for two elderly ladies to live in!

The Spry sisters were twins. Mandy didn't know how old they were exactly but they looked ancient. They lived at The Riddings all alone except for Geoffrey, the gardener.

Geoffrey was even more ancient than the sisters. He hardly ever set foot inside the house. Then there was Patch, the kitten the Spry sisters had

26

adopted when Mandy and James were looking for homes for four kittens.

'Will they let us in?' said James.

'Of course they will,' said Mandy. 'They took Patch in, didn't they? They wouldn't turn away a wounded animal.'

Mrs Hope brought the four-wheel drive to a stop just as the front door opened. Miss Marjorie Spry peered round the door. 'Have you forgotten something, Mrs Hope?' she said nervously, her hands pulling at the ancient cardigan she wore.

Emily Hope got out of the car and opened the door for James to get out with the vixen. 'No,' she said. 'But we have a wounded fox here and we need your help.'

'Our help?' said another voice and Miss Joan appeared behind her sister.

Mandy held her breath. Then, between the feet of Miss Joan, a little cat appeared.

'Patch!' said Mandy. 'How is he?'

Miss Marjorie smiled. 'Your mother said it was nothing to worry about,' she said. 'Just a little cold. But you can't be too careful, can you?'

Mrs Hope smiled back. 'No, indeed,' she said, and waited while Miss Marjorie and Miss Joan looked at each other and then at James with the vixen in his arms.

'It's so good of you to come and see Patch here,' said Miss Marjorie to Mrs Hope.

'We don't go out much,' finished Miss Joan.

'So I think, since you are always so understanding . . .' said Miss Marjorie.

'. . . we must do all we can for you,' said Miss Joan.

It was amazing how they finished each other's sentences, Mandy thought.

'Come in,' said Miss Marjorie, holding the door wide.

Mandy heaved a sigh of relief and cuddled the cub in her jumper. 'Oh, thank you,' she said. 'Thank you so much.'

'We'd like to use your kitchen,' said Emily Hope. 'And we have no time to lose.' Already she was hurrying into the house, Mandy and James and the twin sisters following her.

The kitchen was vast and old-fashioned. Mandy's mother cleared a space on the kitchen table and laid a polythene sheet from her bag over it. Mandy watched her mother proudly.

At once Emily Hope was businesslike, ordering water to be boiled, unpacking her bag, setting everything out on the kitchen table. At last she was ready.

'Mandy,' she said, 'you'll have to help me. I'm going to stitch the wound in the leg first but she might need some more treatment. We'll have to see. That birth couldn't have been easy for her.'

Mandy nodded and handed the cub to James. Immediately the Spry sisters clustered round.

'Oh, how tiny,' said Miss Marjorie. 'And look at those little ears—all tightly curled up.'

'We must find something to put it in,' said Miss Joan. 'Come with us, young man.'

James set the cub carefully down on the table. It moved slightly, snuggling into Mandy's warm jumper. As he followed the sisters out of the kitchen,

James looked back.

'Go on,' said Mandy. 'We'll look after the cub.'

Mandy watched her mum scrub up at the kitchen sink, then put on rubber gloves. She took a spray from her bag and sprayed the vixen's leg.

'A local anaesthetic to freeze the wound is all I dare risk,' she said to Mandy. She pointed to her stethoscope. 'Take that, Mandy, and listen to her breathing for me while I work. If there's any change let me know at once.' She looked down at her patient. 'And if I need you down here I'll tell you.'

Mandy went to the vixen's head and began to stroke it. The vixen's eyes were still closed. She looked very weak and small. Mandy put the stethoscope on. It wasn't the first time she had used one; her dad had shown her how to listen for a heartbeat, how to detect changes in breathing. The vixen's heartbeat seemed steady.

As her mum worked, Mandy listened to the vixen's heart. From time to time she spoke to the animal, gently, calming. Once the fox opened her eyes and Mandy saw the fright in them. She looked over at her mum. Emily Hope was bent over her patient.

'Not long now,' Mandy said to the vixen. 'It'll soon be over.'

'Mandy,' said Emily Hope, 'come and help.'

Mandy took the wad of gauze Mrs Hope was holding out.

'Just dab it as I work,' said Mrs Hope.

Mandy looked at the neat row of stitches her mother had put in the vixen's leg. There was blood at the edges of the wound. Mandy dabbed as her mother put in the last few stitches.

'How is she?' said Mandy.

Her mother shook her head. 'The leg wound should be OK,' she said. 'But I want to get her down to Animal Ark for a thorough investigation. After all, she's just had cubs and she's weak and in shock. She'll need an injection against infection and a lot of tender loving care.'

Mandy smiled. 'I can give her that,' she said.

Mandy's mother smiled back. 'If the vixen pulls through you'll be busy enough looking after her cub,' she said.

Just at that moment James came back into the kitchen with the Spry sisters. He was carrying a cat basket. Inside the basket was a scrap of blue blanket. Gently, he lifted the cub and placed him in the basket on top of the blanket.

'Why, that's perfect for carrying him!' said Emily Hope.

The sisters beamed. 'He's so tiny. James told us what happened, Mandy. Nasty wicked things, gin traps. Father never used them,' Miss Joan said.

'Father used to hunt foxes,' said Miss Marjorie. 'He used to say that at least that way you got a bit of sport.'

'But Father did *not* approve of traps,' Miss Joan said.

Mandy opened her mouth to say that she thought fox-hunting was cruel, then she closed it again. The Spry sisters had been so kind, letting them use their kitchen, providing a basket for the cub—even a blanket to keep him warm.

And the cub and his mother were safe now. That was all that mattered.

CHAPTER THREE

The journey to Animal Ark was a lot less worrying than the one to The Riddings had been. At least the vixen had stopped bleeding.

'She isn't out of danger yet, though,' said Emily Hope. 'I'd like to see what Dad says.'

As they drew up to Animal Ark, Adam Hope was coming round the corner of the house from the surgery. He was wearing a track suit; he had taken to jogging to try and get his weight down. His dark hair was tousled from his run.

Mandy looked at the old, stone cottage with the wooden sign that said

'Animal Ark, Veterinary Surgeon' swinging in the breeze. Banks of flowers bordered the path and the stone flags glowed mellow in the sunlight. She loved her home. Already, she felt the fox and cub were safer just because they were here.

'Hi, you lot,' called Adam Hope, coming towards them and smiling his special lop-sided smile. Even his beard couldn't hide that smile. 'What have you got there?'

Mandy opened the cat basket and showed him, while James told the story of finding the vixen.

Mr Hope's eyes darkened as he listened. 'Disgusting things these traps,' he said as he took the vixen from his wife. He began to carry it round to the surgery. 'They're illegal for a start, and dangerous to all kinds of animals.'

'And to children,' said Mrs Hope. 'Can you imagine a small child coming across one of those? It doesn't bear thinking about.'

'Should we tell the police?' James said. 'They could find out who set the trap, couldn't they?'

Mr Hope shook his head. 'Whoever set this isn't going to admit to the police that they did it,' he said. 'And anyway, there could be other traps.'

'You mean more foxes could be getting trapped in these horrible things?' said Mandy. 'Then we *should* tell the police. They could search for them.'

They were at the surgery entrance now and Emily Hope pushed open the door. 'Unless you knew exactly where to look, it would be a waste of time,' she said. 'You could look for weeks and never find it. The police don't have time for that kind of thing. Even if the people who set the traps are caught, they will only get fined. It won't stop them doing it.'

'My goodness, what have you got there?' said a voice from behind the reception desk. Jean Knox, the receptionist, peered at them. She caught hold of the glasses that were dangling from a chain round her neck and put them on. 'Good heavens,' she said as she saw the new patients.

'A fox and her cub, Jean,' said Dad.

'We're just going to give the vixen a thorough check-up now. Mandy and James will settle the cub in the residential unit.' He turned to Mandy. 'Don't forget to put him in the annex,' he said.

Mandy nodded. The annex was a little room at the back of the residential unit. It had recently been set up for the wild animals that sometimes had to be treated at Animal Ark.

'Simon is in the surgery,' Jean said.

Mandy looked at James as her mum and dad disappeared into the surgery. 'The vixen will be OK,' James said reassuringly.

'I hope so,' said Mandy looking down at the cat basket. The cub was beginning to stir. 'If she doesn't survive, the cub won't either.'

'Come on,' said James. 'Let's get him settled.' And he held open the door to the unit.

Mandy nodded. 'We'll need a cage big enough for both of them,' she said.

'It's a pity they can't be with the other animals,' James said.

Mandy shook her head. 'You know how careful we have to be about cross-infection,' she said. 'Mum and Dad always keep the wild animals separate from the domestic ones.'

They found a large cage and Mandy laid the cub in it, tucking his blanket round him. The little animal barely stirred while she did it.

'He's fast asleep again,' said James.

Mandy sighed. 'I suppose he'll be getting hungry soon,' she said. 'James, what if his mother isn't well enough to feed him?'

James turned from the cage. 'It'll be all right,' he said. 'You'll see. Your mum and dad are terrific vets.' He smiled. 'Tell you what, let's go and visit the other animals.'

Mandy smiled back. 'OK,' she said, 'Let's start with the cats. But first we'll have to wash our hands after handling the cub.'

James and Mandy made a complete tour of the unit. It was certainly better than just waiting around brooding. As well as the cats, there were a couple of guinea-pigs who snuffled at the bars of their cage as Mandy approached.

'Hello, Tig and Tag,' Mandy said to the guinea pigs. They were waiting to be collected by their new owner. She popped a couple of carrots into their cage as a treat.

Poor Jilly,' said James, standing beside a cage with a very sorry-looking puppy in it. 'What's wrong with her?'

'She's just had her injections,' Mandy said, 'and she didn't like them much.'

Jilly woofed softly and came and licked James's hand through the wire of her cage. James gave in. 'OK,' he said. 'Let's give you a cuddle then,' and he lifted the puppy out of the cage and brought her over to Mandy.

Mandy was standing beside a cage with a tortoise in it.

'She's got something wrong with her eye,' Mandy said to James. 'But she's getting better.'

'Of course she is,' said James. 'With your mum and dad looking after her, she's bound to get better.'

Mandy looked at James standing there holding the puppy. 'And I feel better too,' she said. 'Thanks, James.'

James flushed. 'No problem,' he said. He went to put Jilly back in her cage to hide his embarrassment.

The door to the unit opened and Mr Hope came in.

Mandy held her breath. 'Will the vixen get better?' she said.

Her dad nodded but she could see a line of worry round his mouth.

'There are some complications,' he said. 'Mum thought there would be. The vixen wasn't quite ready to have her cubs. She'll need to stay here for a few weeks. There's no way she's fit to be out in the wild yet.'

'So the cub will be all right?' said Mandy.

Emily Hope came in with Simon behind her carrying the vixen. Mandy and James followed them through to the annex where the foxes' cage was.

'She might have a bit of bother feeding the cub,' said Emily Hope. 'You two will have to help.'

'Oh, we'll do anything. Won't we, James?' said Mandy eagerly.

Mandy's mother laughed. 'Let's see if you say that when you're in here every few hours trying to top up the cub's feed,' she said.

'We'll take it in turns,' said James, but Mandy didn't mind how often she had to feed the cub. The vixen was going to survive. She and James would look after the cub.

Simon bent down and laid the vixen next to her cub. At once the tiny scrap snuggled up and nuzzled for a feed.

'She doesn't have a lot of milk,' said Emily Hope.

'It's just as well she only has the one cub to feed,' said Adam Hope. He turned to Mandy. 'Mum told me about the other cubs,' he said. 'I'll go up there now and attend to things. You know, Mandy,' he added very gently, 'if she was trying to feed more than one cub she would never manage it. It would put all their lives at risk. She'll have a hard enough job feeding that one.'

'She's so small,' said Mrs Hope, 'but it's lucky for her she is. If her leg hadn't been so slender it would have been smashed in that trap and beyond repair.'

Simon grinned at them all. 'I'd say it was this little fellow that was lucky,' he said, tickling the cub under the chin. 'Lucky that you two came along.'

Mandy smiled down at the mother and baby snuggled up closely together. 'Then that's what we'll call the cub,' she said. 'We'll call him Lucky.'

*　　　*　　　*

The next two weeks were incredibly busy for Mandy. Mrs Hope had been right when she said Mandy would have her work cut out for her. The vixen was still weakened by her ordeal, but she was managing to feed Lucky a little each day and Mandy soon learned to top up the cub's diet with warm milk. At first, she had to use a doll's feeding-bottle. Then Lucky grew big enough to manage a baby's feeding-bottle. Then, on the eleventh day, his eyes opened.

'They're blue!' Mandy said to James when he made his regular afternoon visit to the foxes.

Lucky looked up at the sound of her voice and yawned. Mandy yawned too and James laughed. 'You're tired,' he said.

'It's been hard work,' said Mandy. 'But that doesn't matter.' She stifled another yawn. 'Look, James. I thought his eyes would be brown.'

The cub's blue-grey eyes blinked up at them sleepily before they closed again and he curled up, asleep.

'Aren't you proud of him?' said Mandy to Lucky's mother. The vixen was still very weak. But there was a brightness in her eyes that hadn't been there a week ago. 'Come on,' Mandy said to James. 'Let's tell Mum.'

They found Mrs Hope clearing up after surgery.

'Great news,' she said when they told her. 'Of course his eyes will turn brown in time.' She smiled. 'He's making really good progress. And so is his mother.'

As Lucky grew bigger Mandy began to give him bread soaked in milk and honey. At two weeks he began to take notice of what was going on round about him, and after another week he was eating solid food and exploring his cage. Mandy let him out for a little while each day and soon he was into everything, tumbling round the floor and getting up to mischief.

'He's quite a handful,' Simon said to Mandy one day, as he was doing the medications.

Mandy laughed. She was giving the foxes' cage a thorough clean. Mother and cub were on the floor, Lucky romping around his mother, trying to get her to play with him.

'She still isn't completely better,' said Mandy, looking at the vixen.

Mr Hope came in with a small

bundle in his arms. 'I want this puppy to stay overnight just to keep an eye on him,' he said to Simon. He looked at the foxes. 'You know, Mandy, I think it's time to separate Lucky from his mother. She isn't really up to all this romping around. And now that he's on solid food he doesn't need to be near her all the time.'

Mandy nodded. 'That's true. He eats anything,' she said.

Mr Hope laughed. 'That's one thing about foxes,' he said. 'They aren't too fussy about what they eat. Rabbits, hedgehogs, birds—as well as any kitchen scraps they can find.'

Mandy smiled. 'Lucky likes honey and sponge cake best,' she said.

'I hope that isn't all you give him,' Mr Hope said.

'Oh, no,' said Mandy. 'He can manage stewed apples and minced beef and all kinds of things.'

'I'm glad to hear it,' Mr Hope said. 'But I'd like his mother's appetite to improve. She's still far from well.'

Mandy bit her lip. 'Maybe Lucky tires her too much,' she said. 'Should I put him in a separate cage?'

Mr Hope smiled. 'If he'll stay there,' he said. 'Foxes are very good at getting out of things like cages. But you can try.'

Mandy grinned. 'He's adorable, isn't he?' she said.

'Adorable,' said her dad as Lucky loped over to him and started trying to nip his ankle.

There was a voice outside and the sound of bicycle wheels on gravel. Mandy turned. 'That's James,' she said. 'We're going on a bike ride.'

'Put Lucky back first,' said Mr Hope. 'If you can catch him.'

Lucky was scampering across the floor. Occasionally he would over-balance and roll over. 'I can catch him. I can run faster than he can,' said Mandy.

Her dad grinned back. 'Give him a couple of weeks,' he said, 'and then watch him run. That little fellow is going to be a holy terror.'

She scooped Lucky up off the floor and put him and his mother back in their cage.

Mr Hope reached for another cage. 'Put the cub in here. Give the poor vixen a bit of a rest.' He paused. 'There's another reason,' he said.

Mandy looked at him. 'What?' she said.

'Well,' said Mr Hope. 'The vixen is getting a bit better now. She notices what's going on around her. I don't want her to get too used to us. You see, if she loses her fear of human beings she might have trouble surviving in the wild.'

'You mean I have to stay away from her?' Mandy said.

'It's hard, I know,' said Mr Hope. 'But the less she's fussed over, the better it will be for her in the end. After all, when we release her, she has to teach Lucky to look after himself And she can't do that if she trusts humans too much.'

Mandy frowned. 'But we would never hurt them,' she said.

'No,' said Mr Hope slowly. 'But other people might. Remember the trap?'

Mandy frowned. 'Does that mean I

can't look after Lucky either?' she said.

'No,' said Mr Hope. 'He's young and he'll learn from his mother once we release him. But you can't make a pet of him. It wouldn't be fair.'

Mandy transferred the cub and his blanket to the cage her dad was holding open. Lucky was very fond of his blanket. She snapped down the latch and looked at the cub. She would miss him when he was gone. But he was a wild animal and Mandy knew that Dad was right.

James came in just as Mandy finished washing her hands. He had Blackie with him. The Labrador's tail was wagging so hard it looked as if it was about to fly off.

'Hello, Blackie,' Mandy said getting down on her knees and putting her arms round the dog's neck.

Blackie licked her face and wagged his tail even more.

Mandy looked at James. 'Let's forget the bike ride and take Blackie for a good long walk,' she said.

James nodded. 'That's just what Mum suggested when he knocked over

48

her favourite vase and broke it. You don't mind, do you?'

Mandy grinned. Blackie was the friendliest dog in the world but he was also accident-prone and disobedient.

At that moment her mother came into the unit. 'Emergency,' she said to Mr Hope. 'There's a cow calving up at Twyford and it's in trouble. I have to go.' She looked at Mandy. 'I've got some medicine for Patch,' she said. 'Would you deliver it for me? I promised the Sprys I'd get it to them this afternoon.'

Mandy nodded eagerly. 'I've been wanting to go and thank them for what they did for the foxes,' she said. 'Of course we'll go, won't we, James?'

James nodded. 'Sure,' he said. 'Mackie can still get his walk. If we don't go too fast he can run along beside us. He loves doing that.'

Mandy's mum handed her a small bottle of eardrops. 'It's his ears again,' she said. 'Tell the sisters not to worry. One drop in each ear morning and night and Patch will be as fit as a fiddle in a few days.'

'I'll tell them,' said Mandy as she put the bottle in her pocket. Then she turned to James. 'Race you,' she said and she was out of the door and on her bike before he had time to reply.

James caught up with her at the corner by the Fox and Goose. They pedalled peacefully along together, not going too fast for Blackie's sake. The Labrador was having a wonderful time investigating the hedgerows and ditches and loping off over the wall that bordered the road. Mandy could see his black, plumy tail waving above the long grass of Redpath's field as they came round by the church. James whistled and Blackie gave an answering bark, but he didn't come to heel.

'That dog *never* listens,' Mandy laughed.

James shook his head ruefully. 'Don't I know it!' he said. 'I just wish I could persuade Mum it's not worth trying. She thinks I should take him to obedience classes!'

'What obedience classes?' said Mandy.

James looked miserable. 'Mrs

50

Ponsonby's,' he said. 'She's advertising them at the village hall. Mum heard about it when she was at the WI last week.'

Mandy gaped. Mrs Ponsonby was a very large, very determined woman who liked to think she ran the whole village. She had blue-rinsed hair and pink spectacles and a voice like a foghorn. She also had two dogs, a Pekinese called Pandora and a mongrel called Toby.

'I suppose she's all right really,' Mandy said. 'I mean she took Toby in when he had no home.' Mandy thought of the poor abandoned little puppy. 'But I still wouldn't want to go to her obedience classes,' she said. 'And anyway Blackie's just—well, Blackie,' she finished and grinned at James.

'That's just it,' said James. 'I like Blackie just the way he is. I don't want anybody to change him.'

Mandy lifted her head. 'In that case,' she said, 'we've got to make sure Blackie doesn't go to those obedience classes.'

'How are we going to do that?' said

51

James.

Mandy shrugged. 'Something will turn up,' she said. 'It's bound to. I mean, can you imagine that dog *ever* listening to you?'

CHAPTER FOUR

When they got to The Riddings there was a car drawn up in front of the house. Mandy recognised the driver.

'It's Dennis Saville,' she said to James.

James grimaced. Dennis Saville worked for Sam Western, who owned the most modern farm in the district. Neither Mandy nor James liked Dennis Saville or Sam Western. In fact, they had good cause to dislike them quite a lot after the two men had tried to poison a goat belonging to a friend of theirs.

'He's got the dogs with him,' James said as Dennis Saville got out of the car and opened the back door to let two bulldogs out.

Mandy looked at the powerful dogs. She loved all animals but these dogs had been trained to be suspicious and unfriendly. It wasn't the dogs' fault. It was their owner's.

Blackie came loping out of the trees that grew almost up to the driveway and the two bulldogs growled.

'Here, Blackie,' James said quickly.

Blackie didn't stop. He trotted up to the two bulldogs, his tongue hanging out, grinning in a friendly fashion.

The bulldogs snarled and Dennis Saville caught their collars.

'Call your dog!' he said sharply to James.

James got off his bike and went and grabbed Blackie's collar. He clipped on the lead and almost had to drag him away from the other two dogs. Blackie seemed to be wondering why he couldn't have a nice game with the bulldogs.

'Keep him tied up,' said Dennis Saville, shortly. 'If you know what's good for him, that is!' And he strode off down the drive with the bulldogs at his heels.

'What a cheek,' said Mandy. 'You'd think he owned the place.'

She stroked Blackie. 'Poor Blackie; you're so friendly, aren't you?'

James was red with embarrassment and annoyance. 'Maybe Mum's right,' he said. 'Maybe Blackie does need obedience classes.'

Mandy's mouth set firmly. 'I like him just as he is,' she said. 'Let's deliver those eardrops and get out of here.'

It was Miss Marjorie who opened the door.

'We've brought Patch's eardrops,' said Mandy. 'Mum says he'll be fine in a day or two and not to worry.'

But Miss Marjorie looked very worried indeed. She took the eardrops gratefully. 'That was kind of you,' she said. But Mandy could tell her mind was on something else.

'Is anything wrong, Miss Marjorie?' she asked.

Miss Marjorie put her hand to her head. 'It's so confusing,' she said, 'and I'm sure we don't want to be spoilsports, but really we don't know what to tell him.'

'Who?' said Mandy.

'Why, Mr Western of course,' said Miss Marjorie. 'He's with Joan now.'

Mandy looked at her. 'What does Mr Western want?' she said.

Miss Marjorie looked surprised. 'Why, he wants to start a fox-hunt,' she said. 'Didn't I say? But, of course, he needs our permission to hunt over our land.'

Mandy was horrified. 'You won't let him, will you, Miss Marjorie?' she said.

Miss Marjorie looked doubtful. 'Dear Papa always used to hunt,' she said.

'But it's wrong,' said Mandy. 'Fox-hunting is cruel.'

James caught her arm as a figure emerged from the dining-room. He had grey-blond hair combed carefully into a quiff and he wore very smart tweeds. 'I shall expect your answer very soon, Miss Joan,' he was saying to the other twin.

Miss Joan fluttered her hands. 'Really, Mr Western, I don't know,' she was saying.

Sam Western turned to her. 'Just think what your father would say,' he said. '*He* wouldn't have any doubts.'

Miss Joan fluttered her hands again. 'But neither Marjorie nor I ever liked fox-hunting,' she said.

Mr Western looked down at her sternly. 'Your father would be ashamed of you,' he said. And he turned and marched straight past Mandy and James, hardly looking at them.

Mandy watched as he strode out of the door. She turned to Miss Joan. 'You can't let him do it,' she said. 'It's so cruel.'

'Oh, dear,' said Miss Joan. 'Marjorie, whatever are we to do?'

Mandy looked at the sisters. 'Just tell him,' she said. 'Tell him he can't hunt on your land.'

Miss Marjorie pursed her lips. 'How can we?' she said. 'He isn't the sort of person you can "just tell".'

Mandy frowned. Miss Marjorie was right. Sam Western wasn't the type to listen to something he didn't want to hear and the sisters were far too timid to deal with him.

There was only one thing to do. She grabbed James's arm. 'We've got to go now,' she said to the sisters, as she hurried James out of the door. 'Give our love to Patch.'

'Where are we going in such a rush?' said James.

Mandy's face was grim. 'If the sisters can't persuade him it's wrong then we have to,' she said.

'Mr Western?' said James. 'I don't fancy our chances.'

But Mandy wasn't listening. They had reached the bottom of the steps and Sam Western was just getting into his car. Dennis Saville was holding the car door open for him. The dogs were already in the back. Mr Western was speaking to Dennis Saville, his voice quite clear. Mandy shrank back behind the stone balustrade and pulled James with her. 'Listen,' she whispered.

'And if I lay my hands on whoever sprang that trap they'll be sorry, believe me,' he was saying.

Dennis Saville nodded. 'At least the other one is untouched,' he said. 'Why on earth would anybody bother with them? Foxes are nothing but vermin.'

Mandy felt her face go white. She grasped James's arm as Mr Western got into the car and drove away.

'Did you hear that?' she said to James. 'They're the ones who set that trap! *And* they've laid another one!'

'You'll never persuade him to give up this idea of fox-hunting,' James said. 'Did you hear what he said about foxes being vermin?'

Mandy nodded. She thought of Lucky and his mother. How could anybody call them vermin? How could anybody lay such cruel traps for animals? She turned to James, her face determined.

'There's nothing we can do,' said James before she could speak. 'Except maybe try and make the Spry sisters stand up to him.'

Mandy nodded again. 'We can try that,' she said. 'But there's something else we have to do first.'

'What's that?' said James.

'We have to find that other trap before some other poor animal is caught in it.'

James shook his head slowly. 'That won't be easy,' he said. 'It could be anywhere. Remember what your dad said.'

'I know,' said Mandy, 'but we've got to try, James. Just think if another animal got caught. We might not be there to rescue it.'

James was looking at the powerful car as it swept down the drive and out through the gates. 'OK,' he said. 'We'll try. And if anybody can do it we can.'

Mandy's face was determined. 'We'll beat him yet,' she said. 'Just see if we don't.'

But when they got back to Animal Ark they found they had another problem on their hands.

Mandy looked round the residential unit. Bedding was strewn across the floor, a couple of feeding dishes were overturned and Lucky was nowhere to be seen.

'Where is he?' she said to Jean, who was in the middle of clearing up.

Jean shook her head. 'Disappeared,' she said.

'But how did he get out?' said Mandy. 'I fastened the cage. I know I did.'

Mr Hope turned from where he was renewing a dressing on a kitten's leg. 'They don't talk about being cunning as a fox for nothing, Mandy,' he said. 'My guess is he slipped the latch on his cage. He's a clever little thing.'

Mandy breathed a sigh of relief. 'You aren't angry then?' she said.

Mr Hope grinned. 'There isn't any point in being angry,' he said. 'It's in a fox cub's nature to be mischievous, and his mother isn't well enough yet to keep him in line.'

Mandy looked at the vixen. She was lying peacefully in her cage. Her leg was mending well enough but her coat was dull and she was very thin. 'We'll find Lucky, Dad.'

'But where?' said James.

Mr Hope laughed. 'Don't worry too much about that,' he said. 'Lucky is still too young to want to go too far away from his mother. But in a week or so . . .'

'What?' said Mandy.

Mr Hope put the kitten back in his cage and came over to them. 'It's the other animals I'm worried about,' he said. 'If Lucky can open his own cage he can open others. Some of the animals are still pretty ill. There's also the risk of cross-infection. We can't let wild animals come into close contact with domestic animals.'

Mandy's heart was sinking. 'But the vixen isn't well enough to be released into the wild yet,' she said. 'You said it would be another two weeks at least.'

Mr Hope nodded. 'That's true,' he

said. 'But Lucky is already on solid food. In a week or so he should be weaned completely. That will be good for his mother. She can use all her strength to get better.'

'And Lucky?' said Mandy. 'You can't let Lucky go all on his own. He's far too little.'

Mr Hope shook his head. 'I wasn't thinking that,' he said. 'But I don't think he can stay here.'

'So where is he to go?' said Mandy.

Mr Hope smiled gently. 'I think that's up to you and James,' he said. 'You'll have to find another home for him until he and his mother can be released together. I'm sorry, Mandy, but it has to be. Once Lucky's got a taste for freedom there will be no holding him. You must see I can't risk the welfare of the other animals.'

Mandy nodded miserably. Where were they going to find another home for Lucky? If he caused trouble at Animal Ark he would cause trouble anywhere.

'Meanwhile . . .' Mr Hope began.

'Yes?' said Mandy.

Her dad grinned. 'Don't you think you'd better go and see if you can find him?'

'Cripes,' said James and Mandy gasped.

'Where shall we start?' she said, looking at James.

James looked just as lost as she felt. One way and another the problems just seemed to be piling up. First the fox-hunting, then the other trap and now losing Lucky. Life was very complicated!

*   *   *

They found him at last in the pantry. Emily Hope was holding him gently and scolding him—but not too harshly. 'Is this what you're looking for?' she said, her green eyes dancing.

Mandy nodded, gathering the naughty fox cub into her arms. 'Dad says we have to find another home for him,' she said.

Mrs Hope pursed her lips. 'It might not be a bad idea,' she said. 'Just until they're both fit to be let go. If he stays

here, he's in danger of turning into a family pet. That isn't a good idea for a wild animal.'

Mandy nodded. 'That's what Dad says,' she said. 'But where can he go? Who would take him?'

Mrs Hope shook her head. 'You'd need somebody patient, who likes animals, doesn't mind a mess around the place and doesn't mind feeding him regularly.' She sniffed and laughed and said, 'And doesn't mind giving him the occasional bath—which is what I think you two had better do now.'

Mandy looked at her hands. 'Where has he been?' she said.

Emily Hope laughed. 'Oh, in the butter, in the jam, and he managed to knock a bag of sugar over himself.'

James grinned. 'I'll get a basin of water and some soap.'

'And I'll just go and help Dad with the dressings,' said Mrs Hope. 'Something tells me Lucky isn't going to like being bathed very much.'

Mandy held the cub up and looked at him severely. 'Now how are we going to find a home for you if you're so naughty?' she said.

The little cub yawned and tried to nip her finger.

'Rascal,' said Mandy as James came back with a basin full of soapy water and an apron for each of them. 'Just see what happens when you get into such a state!'

Mandy and James were soaked by the time they had finished.

'Gosh, for such a tiny little thing, he's a handful, isn't he?' said James as Lucky splashed water all over him again.

And that was the trouble, Mandy thought. Who on earth could they ask to take on a load of mischief like Lucky?

CHAPTER FIVE

Mandy and James tried everyone they could think of. But by the middle of the week they still hadn't found a home for Lucky. Either people had enough animals of their own to look after or they were a bit wary of taking in a fox cub. Meanwhile, Lucky was getting even more mischievous as the days went on.

'He got out again this morning,' said Mandy when she met James at the crossroads by the Fox and Goose on Saturday.

'What did he do this time?' said James.

Mandy smiled in spite of herself. 'He got into the flour bin,' Mandy said. 'He seems to like the pantry.'

'I wonder why,' said James, grinning. 'Have you seen this?'

Mandy looked. James was pointing to a poster on the front door of the pub. 'GRAND AUCTION' it said. 'In aid of Cub Scout Funds.'

'I heard about that,' said Mandy. 'The Cub Scouts want to buy tents. I must remember to donate something to it.'

'That's what I like to hear,' said a voice. 'Tommy has his heart set on going to Cub camp this summer.'

Mandy turned to see an old man in a flat cloth cap. It was Walter Pickard. He and Grandad were church bell-ringers together. Walter lived in one of a row of cottages behind the Fox and Goose. Tommy was his great-grandson.

'I hear you've got a fox cub and vixen up at Animal Ark,' the old man went on.

'Oh, Mr Pickard, I don't suppose you could take Lucky in just for a week or so until his mother gets better.'

'Lucky?' said Walter.

Mandy nodded. 'The fox cub. He's getting into mischief and Dad is a bit worried about the other animals.'

Walter shook his head. I'd like to help you, young miss,' he said gently. 'But I don't think Tom and Missie and Scraps would like it.'

Mandy's heart sank. Walter had three cats. Certainly they wouldn't appreciate sharing their home with a fox cub.

'What about your gran and grandad?' said Walter.

'Are they home yet?' said James. 'We thought they were still away.'

'I saw the camper van turning into the lane as I was passing,' said Walter. 'I'm glad to see your grandad back. We've a lot to do to get the auction set up and things collected.'

Mandy and James were already on their bikes, flying towards Lilac Cottage. 'Thanks, Mr Pickard!' Mandy called back.

'Tell your grandad there's bell-ringing practice this afternoon!' Walter called after them. 'I'll see him there!'

*   *   *

Lilac Cottage stood at the end of a lane at the other end of the village. Mandy's grandparents were unloading the camper van as Mandy and James arrived.

'Hi, Gran,' Mandy called, jumping off her bike and throwing herself into her grandmother's arms. Gran hugged her.

'Mandy!' she said breathlessly, 'You'd think we'd been away for a year instead of just two weeks!'

Mandy laughed up into Gran's face. 'You're home early,' she said. 'We thought you were going to be away for longer.'

Gran smiled. 'I got a sudden notion for spring-cleaning,' she said.

Mandy's grandad came out of Lilac Cottage. 'And you know what *that* means,' he said. 'Everything will be topsy-turvy for a week. But once your gran gets a notion for spring-cleaning there's no holding her.'

Gran's eyes twinkled. 'And I saw a lovely three-piece suite in York when we stopped off for lunch,' she said.

Grandad laughed. 'She didn't just

see it. It's being delivered on Thursday,' he said. 'And a new china cabinet.'

Gran tutted. 'We need a new china cabinet,' she said. 'That old one is on its last legs.'

'So am I,' joked Grandad. 'Are you going to get a new one of me?'

Mandy laughed. 'Oh, Grandad,' she said. 'There could only ever be one of you.'

Grandad winked at her and Mandy smiled. Gran tutted. 'Last legs indeed,' she said to Grandad. 'You're as fit as a fiddle.'

'You're only saying that because you want me to help with your spring-cleaning,' Grandad said to Gran.

Mandy shook her head. It was good to have them home again.

'We've got to get the house in apple pie order for the new furniture,' said Gran.

James looked at Mandy hopelessly and Mandy's face fell as she saw what he was thinking. With spring-cleaning going on and new furniture, Gran wouldn't want a mischievous fox cub running around.

'Lost a pound and found a penny?' Grandad said to her when he saw her glum face.

Mandy explained their problem. Grandad shook his head. 'A fox cub?' he said. 'That's a hard one all right. I don't see many people taking on a bundle of trouble like that.'

'Cubs,' said Gran suddenly. 'That reminds me. Young Tommy Pickard was telling me the Cubs are having a fund-raising auction at the village hall next week.' She looked at Grandad. 'I'll give them the old suite,' she said. 'There's a few good years left in it yet.'

Grandad winked at Mandy. 'That isn't what she said in the shop,' he said.

Mandy laughed. 'Even if you can't take the cub it's still good to have you home,' she said. 'Oh, and Walter Pickard says he's glad you're home as well—to help with the auction. And you have bell-ringing practice this afternoon,' she added.

'At this rate I'll need another holiday,' Grandad said. But Mandy could see he was still concerned about her problem. 'Let's go inside and talk about what you're going to do with this cub,' he said.

'I'll put the kettle on,' said Gran. 'A cup of tea always makes you feel better. You'll find somebody to help, Mandy. You've never failed yet.'

'Oh, and another thing, Grandad,' Mandy said as they all trooped into the cottage. 'Mr Western has been setting traps for foxes.'

Her grandad looked at her serious face. 'What?' he said. 'Maybe you'd better tell us all about this.'

Mandy and James told their story over a cup of tea in the kitchen. 'So you see,' Mandy finished. 'If the Sprys let him, he'll start fox-hunting. Meantime, he's setting traps.'

'The Sprys are such gentle people,' said Gran. 'They wouldn't want anything to do with fox-hunting.'

'They said their father loved hunting,' said James. 'Mr Western has really got at them. He says their father would be ashamed of them if they didn't let him use their land.'

'Stuff and nonsense!' said Gran,

74

pouring another cup of tea all round.

Grandad shook his head. 'I remember old Major Spry,' he said. 'He had those girls under his thumb. Sam Western's playing a clever game there.' He looked serious. 'The thing is, I don't like this idea of traps. Anything could get caught in them.'

'That's what *we* thought,' said Mandy. 'We've been looking for the other one but it's like looking for a needle in a haystack!'

Grandad smiled. 'First look for the kind of place you'd find foxes,' he said. 'I don't hold much for Dennis Saville and his like, but he knows his job. He won't have set those traps just anywhere.'

'Where would you look?' said Mandy.

Grandad rubbed his chin. 'Not up on the moors,' he said, 'nor on farmland. They'd be in woodland most probably.'

James nodded. 'That's where the last one was. In Monkton Spinney,' he said.

Grandad nodded. 'That's where I'd look,' he said. Then his face grew serious. 'But if you do find it, stay well away. Don't try anything silly. You could have been badly hurt instead of just getting a scrape, Mandy.'

'That's right,' said Gran. 'You stay well away from it and report back. Grandad and Walter will see to it.'

Mandy nodded obediently but she couldn't help wondering what would have happened to Lucky if she and James had stayed away from the last trap. The telephone rang then and Gran went to answer it while Grandad and Mandy and James talked over their problem. When she came back Gran was frowning. 'That's a pest,' she said.

'What?' said Mandy.

'Amelia Ponsonby has written out a list of stuff to be donated for the auction,' Gran said. 'She wants somebody to go over to Bleakfell Hall and collect it.'

'What's wrong with giving you the list over the phone?' said Grandad.

Gran grinned. 'She also has a list of suggestions about how the auction should be run,' she said. 'And I wanted to make a start on my spring-cleaning.'

'We'll go,' said Mandy. 'Won't we,

James?'

James made a face. Mrs Ponsonby terrified him. She was like a bulldozer. She just flattened everything in her way if she couldn't get what she wanted.

'OK,' said James, not too happily. Then he grinned. 'Do you think she'd take Lucky? She could give him obedience classes!'

Mandy laughed. 'No way,' she said. 'I feel the same way about Lucky as you do about Blackie. I like him just the way he is!'

*　　　*　　　*

Bleakfell Hall was a big Victorian mansion. It looked like something out of a horror film with its long driveway and the dense trees around it. In fact, the house had been used not so long ago as a film location by a film company.

They were almost halfway down the drive of the Hall when they heard the commotion. It sounded like two dogs barking and yelping.

'What on earth is that?' said James.

Mandy brought her bike to a halt and listened. There was a high-pitched yapping sound followed by a series of low growls. 'It sounds like Pandora,' she said.

'She sounds frightened,' said James.

'And angry,' said Mandy.

Pandora was Mrs Ponsonby's peke. Mrs Ponsonby and Pandora had been together long before she took on Toby.

'If something happens to Pandora Mrs Ponsonby will—' Mandy stopped. She couldn't imagine *what* Mrs Ponsonby would do. She might be a real dragon at times but she adored her dogs.

'Let's go!' said James.

They leaped off their bikes and plunged into the belt of trees that bordered the driveway.

'Over here!' James shouted as the yapping got more and more frenzied.

Mandy bounded after James and almost cannoned into him when he suddenly stopped.

'What is it?' said Mandy. She looked at the scene in front of her. Pandora was yapping and nipping at Toby, who was crouched in front of her. Toby was. circling Pandora, growling fiercely and taking little runs at her, stopping her getting past him.

'Toby!' Mandy shouted.

Toby turned and Pandora took her chance to dash forward. At once Toby was on her, snarling, forcing her back.

Mandy looked at James. 'What on earth is going on?' she said. 'I've never seen Toby behave like this before!'

James shrugged. 'I don't know,' he said. 'But we've got to stop it.'

There was the sound of a voice from the driveway. 'Pandora! Toby!' it called. But neither dog paid attention.

'Mrs Ponsonby,' said Mandy. 'Quick, James. You get Pandora. I'll get Toby.'

They each made a dive for the dogs. Mandy held on to Toby's collar and James scooped Pandora up into his arms where she struggled to get free. Toby continued to bark. They were standing there with the struggling dogs when Mrs Ponsonby appeared through the trees behind them.

She looked at them through her pink spectacles, her blue-rinsed hair

quivering with rage as she saw they were holding her precious pets. 'What on earth do you children think you're doing?' she said in a voice like thunder. 'Put my dogs down at once!'

Mandy and James looked at each other. 'Mrs Ponsonby,' said Mandy, 'you're not going to believe this. Toby was attacking Pandora!'

Mrs Ponsonby's face grew so red she looked as if she was going to burst a blood vessel. 'Toby?' she said. 'Attacking my precious Pandora? What nonsense! How dare you speak of Toby like that? I never heard anything so ridiculous in my life.'

'James,' said Mandy. *'James!'* She felt she needed a bit of support here.

But James was looking the other way. 'There's something over there,' he said.

'Where?' said Mandy.

James nodded to where Toby had been. Mandy frowned. 'What on earth was he up to?' she said.

Then, without further ado she thrust Toby into Mrs Ponsonby's arms and walked over to where he had been making such a fuss. Treading carefully through the long grass beneath the trees she looked down—and gasped. 'It's the trap, James!' she said. 'It's the other trap!'

'What trap?' said Mrs Ponsonby. 'What are you talking about? There are no traps on my land.'

James looked at her. 'Dennis Saville put it there,' he said. 'On Mr Western's orders. To catch foxes.'

For once in her life Mrs Ponsonby was speechless. Then she said. 'On *my* land? That man dared to put a trap on *my* land?'

Mandy heaved a sigh of relief. It was clear Mrs Ponsonby knew nothing about it. 'Toby must have been trying to stop Pandora getting near it,' she said. 'You know how nosy Pandora is.'

Mrs Ponsonby drew herself up. 'Inquisitive,' she said.

Mandy smiled. It was one thing Pandora and Mrs Ponsonby had in common—nosiness.

'Anyway I reckon Toby saved Pandora from getting caught in that trap,' said James.

Mrs Ponsonby looked down at Toby. 'My brave boy,' she said. 'What a clever Toby!'

'The question is what are we going to do about it?' said Mandy.

James was still holding Pandora. The little peke was squirming in his arms, still determined to investigate this strange object. 'Your grandad said to leave it alone and let him know,' he said.

Mandy looked at Pandora. 'She'll be over there if we let her go,' she said. 'No, we've got to do something.' She looked around. There were fallen branches lying under the trees. She picked up the heaviest one she could find.

'What are you going to do?' said James.

Mandy's mouth set. 'Spring it,' she said. 'We can't risk leaving it.'

'Be careful,' James said and Mrs Ponsonby echoed his words. Suddenly her face was crumpled with worry. She didn't look her usual confident self.

Slowly, gently, Mandy approached the trap. Its razor sharp jaws gaped at her. She took the branch in both hands and thrust it between the teeth of the trap. At once there was the sound of tearing grass and the clash of steel as the powerful jaws sprang together, almost cutting the heavy branch in two. Mandy felt the judder of the impact in her arms as the trap snatched the branch from her hands. Then she stood back. 'You can let them go now,' she said. 'It's quite safe.'

'My dear child,' said Mrs Ponsonby. 'You're as white as a sheet.'

Mandy let out a deep breath. 'I'm all right,' she said. 'It's Toby who was the hero.'

Mrs Ponsonby's face was grim. 'When I think of what could have happened to my precious Pandora,' she said. 'I'd like to put that man in a trap! I'd like to put him in a cage. In fact I think I'll ask Ernie Bell to make one specially for him. The nerve of it. Putting a trap on *my* grounds!'

Mandy's face brightened. Ernie Bell. She hadn't thought of Ernie Bell. She looked at James and saw the same thought dawn in his mind.

'Do you think he would do it?' he said.

Mandy grinned. 'He might,' she said. 'He took in that squirrel and if anybody can make a cage that will keep Lucky in, he can. It's worth a try, James.'

Mrs Ponsonby looked from one to the other. 'I've no idea what you two are talking about,' she said. 'You're talking in riddles. You must have got a bigger fright than I thought, Mandy. You'd better come up to the house and have a cup of camomile tea. Then you can tell me what's going on—and get that list for your grandmother.' And she turned and marched away, the dogs at her heels.

Mandy and James grinned at each

other. Mrs Ponsonby was back to her
old self!

CHAPTER SIX

Ernie Bell lived in a little cottage a few doors down from Walter Pickard, behind the Fox and Goose pub. Mandy and James wasted no time in getting there.

'We'll have to be careful how we ask,' said Mandy as they parked their bikes outside his cottage.

Ernie's cottage was a picture of neatness. The flower borders marched in a regimented row up the path to the open front door, the windows sparkled like mirrors and the brass handle and letterbox on the shiny dark green front door glittered like gold in the sun. The front door was propped open with a white, painted stone and the doorstep itself gleamed white as new snow in the sunshine.

'Gosh!' said James. 'When did that happen? Ernie's cottage used to look as if it was going to fall down any minute.'

Mandy giggled. 'Mrs Ponsonby told Ernie she didn't think he could look after himself properly and promised to get him a home help.'

'So Ernie cleaned the cottage up?' said James.

Mandy nodded. 'The very next day he was out with the paint pot and the garden tools. Gran says he told her he would show Mrs Ponsonby a thing or two about looking after the place.'

There was a cat sleeping on the doorstep as they approached the door. It woke up and stretched as it heard them.

'Hello, Tiddles,' said Mandy as she bent to stroke the cat. 'I hope your owner is in a good mood today!'

'It won't be easy to get him to agree,' said James thoughtfully. 'But if anybody can build a cage for Lucky, Ernie can. After all, he used to be a carpenter. And he knows how to look after wild animals. He wouldn't make a pet of Lucky. Look at the run he made for Sammy.'

Sammy was an orphaned squirrel Ernie had rescued. He had made a terrific run for the little animal in his back garden. Underneath his crusty exterior Ernie really did have a heart of gold.

Mandy smiled. 'You know how awkward Ernie can be,' she said.

James nodded. 'Like cleaning the cottage up because Mrs Ponsonby thought he couldn't take care of it?'

'So,' said Mandy, 'we've got to make him think he can't do it. Then he'll want to.'

James grinned. 'We've done that before.'

'And it usually works,' said Mandy.

At that moment a small man with short white hair came round the side of the cottage.

'Just go along with anything I say,' Mandy whispered as Ernie saw them.

'Well, you two,' he said. 'And what are you up to now?'

Mandy smiled. 'Hello, Mr Bell. We weren't up to anything. We thought we'd like to see Sammy if that's all right with you.'

Ernie looked at them a bit suspiciously but he couldn't resist a request to see his squirrel. 'Come round the back then,' he said. 'But don't you go feeding him a lot of nonsense now. Young Tommy Pickard was round here yesterday trying to give him biscuits. I don't hold with that. Animals have to keep to their natural foods.'

Mandy thought of Lucky in the pantry but she said, 'Oh, you're right, Mr Bell. It's really important, especially with a wild animal like Sammy.' She looked at James.

'We didn't come just to see Sammy. We wanted to ask your advice as well, Mr Bell,' James said. 'We've got a bit of a problem with a wild animal at the moment.'

Mandy giggled. James made Lucky sound like a man-eating tiger.

'Oh, you have, have you?' said Ernie Bell. 'And what would that be?'

89

'It's a fox cub, Mr Bell,' Mandy said. 'James and I rescued him and his mother from a trap.'

Ernie Bell looked shocked. 'Don't hold with no traps,' he said. 'Nasty things!'

So far so good, Mandy thought.

They were in Ernie's back garden by this time and James and Mandy stook looking at the run Ernie had made. Sammy the squirrel was scampering to and fro, his eyes bright with curiosity at his visitors.

Isn't he lovely?' said Mandy, going over to stand by the run.

Sammy scampered up the wire towards her and perched on one of the supports, his paws poised, ready for anything she might offer him.

'I haven't got anything for you, Sammy,' Mandy said and she thought the little squirrel looked disappointed.

'So, what's this about a fox cub, then?' said Ernie.

'Poor little thing,' she said. 'He was only just born when we rescued him. But he's coming along fine now. That's part of the trouble.'

'Trouble?' said Ernie Bell.

Mandy sighed and nodded. 'He keeps escaping from his cage,' she said. 'He gets into everything and he's beginning to upset some of the other animals.'

Ernie had bent to feed Sammy a few nuts.

'Don't tell him that,' James said to Mandy in a whisper. 'You'll put him off.'

Mandy just grinned. 'Trust me,' she said. 'You know how stubborn Ernie is.'

'What's that?' said the old man.

Mandy jumped. 'You've made such a lovely run for Sammy,' said Mandy. 'We thought if we had a look at it we might be able to do the same for Lucky.' She looked critically at the neat dovetail joints and the netting. 'Of course we couldn't hope to do just as well as you.'

James backed her up. 'Not with you being such a good carpenter,' he said. 'And knowing how to look after wild animals.'

Ernie laid a hand proudly on the fencing of the run. 'It takes years to learn to make dovetail joints as good as that,' he said.

Mandy sighed, 'I know, Mr Bell,' she said. 'But we've got to try. Lucky is so good at escaping we're afraid we're going to lose him altogether. Dad has said we either have to make him secure or find somewhere else for him to go.'

She held her breath, then took the plunge. This was it. If Ernie didn't fall for this they were wasting their time. 'Of course,' she said carefully, 'I don't suppose anybody could make a run that would keep Lucky in, not even you.'

James looked at her. She could see that he was holding his breath as well.

Ernie straightened up slowly and looked at the two of them. 'I don't know about that,' he said. 'I reckon I'm still as good a carpenter as you'll find in Yorkshire.'

'Oh, we didn't mean you weren't,' said James. 'It's just that it would be such a difficult job.' He turned to Mandy. 'But we've got to try, haven't we, Mandy?'

'Before we lose Lucky,' said Mandy.

'And your dad says he can't stay at Animal Ark?' said Ernie.

'It's the other animals,' said Mandy.

Ernie Bell scratched his chin.

'So if you could just give us a drawing we could try and copy it,' said James.

Ernie was still scratching his chin.

'We know it's difficult,' said Mandy.

'Oh, I don't know,' said James, entering into the spirit of the thing. 'It can't be that difficult, can it? I mean all we have to do is make a really strong box—with airholes in it of course.'

Mandy looked at him in horror before she realised what he was up to.

'I suppose so,' she said slowly. 'It wouldn't be too comfortable for him. I mean, he wouldn't have the kind of home Sammy has but we could surely manage something.'

Ernie's voice exploded in Mandy's ear. 'You can't do a thing like that!' he shouted. 'You can't put a wild creature in a box!'

Mandy and James looked at each other.

'But if you can't manage to do it for

us . . .' said Mandy.

Ernie Bell put his head on one side. 'Can't manage?' he said. 'Can't manage? Who said anything about not being able to manage? There isn't a better carpenter in Yorkshire.' He drew himself up and puffed out his chest. 'You give me a couple of days and then bring that little fellow over here. I'll have a run made for him that he won't get out of. But you mark my words, he'll be comfortable in it. Box indeed! I never heard such nonsense.'

Mandy tried to hide her delight. 'Are you sure, Mr Bell?' she said. 'It will be very difficult.'

'Sure?' he said. 'Never mind a couple of days. You bring him over tomorrow morning and you'll see. Now off you go the two of you while I get my tools. I've got work to do!'

*   *   *

'Ernie Bell?' Mr Hope said when they told him. 'You couldn't have found anybody better, but how did you get him to do it? Ernie's the most awkward

man I know.'

'Oh, we have our ways,' Mandy said, grinning at James.

They were back at Animal Ark, checking on Lucky. He was still in his cage, looking up at them with the scrap of blue blanket in his mouth. He looked adorable. The blanket was a bit the worse for wear though. Every day it seemed to get a little smaller. Lucky was very fond of chewing it.

'He's just like a puppy,' said Mandy.

Her dad laughed. 'He's a lot cleverer than a puppy,' he said. 'But that reminds me!'

He went into the cupboard at the end of the room and brought out a dog's lead and collar. 'I don't see why you shouldn't take him for a walk,' he said. 'Just make sure the collar is tight enough. You don't want him escaping in the village!'

Mandy and James slipped the collar round Lucky's neck and clipped on the lead.

'Taking a fox for a walk,' Mandy said. 'That's new.'

'Maybe it'll tire him out,' Mr Hope said. 'He's been out of that cage twice this morning already.'

'Let's take him to see Gran and Grandad,' Mandy said.

Lucky sat there looking up at them, the remains of his blanket still in his mouth.

James laughed. 'He wants to bring his blanket.'

'Of course he can bring it,' Mandy

said. 'It's his security blanket.'

Adam Hope smiled. 'I don't know if Welford has seen a stranger sight,' he said as they walked off down the path with Lucky on the lead and the scrap of blue blanket dangling from his pointed little mouth.

'Welford will have to get used to it,' Mandy said. 'At least until Lucky's mother is better.' She looked at her dad. 'She is getting better, isn't she?' she said.

Mr Hope smiled. 'Give her a week or so,' he said. 'Remember it isn't like sending a domestic animal home. She's got to forage for food for herself and for Lucky. There won't be anyone to feed her. And she has to protect herself and her cub from predators.'

Mandy's mouth turned down. *And from traps,* she thought.

'We found the other trap,' she said to her dad.

Mr Hope was all ears. 'Where?' he said.

Mandy and James told him the story. He gave them a lecture about being careful of these things before he told them how terrific they were.

'Who's terrific?' said Emily Hope, coming out of the front door of the house.

'We are,' said Mandy. 'Ask Dad.'

Her mum was getting into her car. 'As if I didn't know that already,' she said. 'I've got a call to make at Sunrise Farm. Do you want a lift anywhere?'

Mandy looked down at Lucky. He was twisting his lead round her ankles.

James bent down to untangle it. 'I'd rather take him for that walk,' he said.

'We're taking him to see Gran and Grandad,' she said. 'I've got to give Gran Mrs Ponsonby's list of stuff she's giving for the auction.'

Mrs Hope laughed. 'It'll be worthwhile going to the auction just to see what Mrs Ponsonby is donating,' she said. 'Bleakfell Hall is the most amazing place I've ever seen. Full of weird and wonderful things.'

'Including Mrs Ponsonby,' James muttered and Mandy giggled.

They waved goodbye and started out for Gran and Grandad's. It took them a lot longer than it should have done to get there. It wasn't just that Lucky wanted to investigate every nook and cranny on the way and sniff at every interesting smell, but people asked how the vixen was getting on. News certainly got around in Welford.

It seemed that the whole village knew Lucky's story.

'Mrs Ponsonby must have told everybody,' said James.

'He's famous,' said Mandy as they came out of the post office. The MacFarlanes who ran it had seen them passing and insisted on them coming in to let them see the little animal.

Even Mr Hardy at the pub had come out to have a look and insisted on taking a picture of Lucky. 'After all,' he said, 'it is the *Fox* and Goose!'

'Now all you need is a goose,' laughed Mandy. Mr Hardy patted his camera. 'I'll put this picture up over the bar,' he said. 'If you come across a goose, let me know!'

They got to Lilac Cottage at last.

'So this is Lucky,' Gran said. 'He's so small. What does he eat? We'll have to feed him up.'

'He won't be small for long if he goes on eating at the rate he has been,' said James.

Mandy fished out Mrs Ponsonby's list and handed it to Gran.

'The whole village knows all about him,' she said. 'They think he's wonderful.'

Gran laughed. 'I'm not surprised,' she said. 'Amelia Ponsonby phoned and told me all about that business with the trap and Pandora. She's on the warpath over this trap setting.'

'Good!' said James. 'I hope she catches Mr Western and Dennis Saville.'

Gran laughed again. 'I don't give much for their chances when she sees them again. Now come in and I'll give this list to Tommy to take to the vicar. He's here.'

Mandy and James followed Gran inside. Tommy Pickard was drinking a glass of milk and eating a slice of sponge cake in the kitchen. Tommy was seven and had just joined the Cub Scouts. He was their keenest member and he wore his uniform as often as he could. He was wearing it now.

'Hi, Tommy,' James said. 'How are your hamsters?'

Tommy answered through a mouthful of sponge cake but his eyes were on Lucky and he was down on his knees at once. 'You've got a new puppy,' he said.

'It isn't a puppy; it's a fox cub!' Mandy said.

Tommy looked up at them, his eyes round, as Lucky nibbled at his fingers and pinched the last of his sponge cake.

'A fox cub?' he said, 'A real fox cub. Wow!'

'He's called Lucky,' said Mandy.

Gran poured glasses of milk and cut wedges of sponge cake for them while she told them all about her new furniture.

'And there are a few other things I can get rid of at the same time,' she said.

'Not get rid of—*donate,* Gran,' Mandy said.

Gran's eyes twinkled. 'Donate,' she said.

Mandy looked round her at Gran's old-fashioned furnishings, her lace table-mats, the jars of dried flowers and shiny, brass ornaments. 'Don't change it too much, Gran,' she said. 'I like it just the way it is.'

Gran laughed. 'Wait till you see my new three-piece suite,' she said. 'It's beautiful.'

But Mandy wasn't so sure she would like it. She was used to Gran and Grandad's cottage looking just the way it did. She even liked their three-piece suite with its big, pink cabbage rose pattern—even if the pattern was a bit faded now and there were a few frayed patches here and there.

It was time to go. Mandy looked round.

'Oh, no,' she said. 'Where's Lucky?'

Tommy looked guilty. 'I just unclipped him for a minute,' he said. All the doors are closed. He couldn't get out.'

They looked everywhere. Under the chairs, behind the sideboard.

'Here he is,' said Tommy, peering into the china cupboard.

Mandy looked in. There was Lucky, peacefully asleep with the blanket between his front paws.

'Oh, look,' she said. 'Isn't he lovely?'

Tommy bit his lip. 'Could we have him as a mascot?' he said.

'What?' said Mandy.

'For the auction,' Tommy said. 'After all he's a cub and we're Cub Scouts. He could be a good mascot. And he's called Lucky. He might bring us luck. We need luck to raise the money for the new tents. If we can get enough money to buy tents we can go camping this summer just like real scouts.'

Mandy laughed. She didn't point out that Cubs were wolf cubs and that Lucky was a fox cub.

'Why not?' she said.

Tommy beamed. 'Terrific!' he said. 'I'll go and tell everybody!'

'Don't forget the list!' Gran called after him but Tommy was gone.

Gran looked at the list. 'This is destined never to get to where it's going,' she said. 'I'd better take it down myself.' She laughed.

'What are you laughing at?' Mandy

said, smiling.

Gran looked at her. 'I was just thinking what an odd auction it's going to be. You should see some of the things Amelia Ponsonby is sending in.' Gran held out the list to Mandy.

'A pedal-organ?' Mandy said as her eyes moved down the list.

'And a fox cub for a mascot. I've never heard anything like it,' said Gran. 'It'll certainly be different!'

CHAPTER SEVEN

Ernie Bell had been true to his word. The pen he made for Lucky was well-constructed and roomy, and the little cub seemed to take to it immediately.

'See,' Ernie had said proudly when he showed it to them. 'You don't get workmanship like that these days!'

Mandy stood with Lucky in her arms and looked at the pen. It was strong and secure, with the netting stapled firmly to the frame. 'It's perfect, Mr Bell!' she said.

And when they put Lucky in it he scampered around, exploring. Finally he settled down with his blanket.

James laughed. 'Look at him,' he

said. 'Mandy's right, Mr Bell. It *is* perfect!'

Ernie Bell scratched his chin and grunted. He was embarrassed at this kind of praise but he was clearly pleased that they liked it so much.

'And we can come and see him every day,' James said.

Ernie looked serious. 'You can come,' he said. 'But I won't have you going feeding him all sorts of rubbish.' The little man drew himself up. 'That there's a wild animal. And you've got to respect that.'

Mandy smiled. They had found the perfect person to look after Lucky.

*　　　*　　　*

Mandy and James went every day to Ernie's cottage. After a day or two, word got round the village. Soon Ernie's back garden was full of children coming to see the fox cub. Ernie harrumphed a lot and complained, but Mandy could tell he liked it really.

Tommy Pickard brought a sign to hang on the pen. 'LUCKY', it said, 'WELFORD CUB SCOUTS' MASCOT.'

'You're famous, Lucky!' Mandy said to the little cub on the day before the auction. Ernie had grudgingly allowed Mandy and James to take Lucky to visit Gran and Grandad.

When they got there, Gran was in a whirl of activity with her spring-cleaning. Mandy and James helped her shift furniture and carry rugs and cushions outside. They got the job of shaking the rugs and beating the cushions.

Lucky, tethered to the gate-post, watched them curiously. He was growing into a fine-looking cub. His

coat was reddish-brown now, his eyes alert, and he made little barking sounds when he was excited. But he was still young enough to need a lot of sleep and he curled up in Gran's old china cupboard with his blanket, while Gran gave Mandy and James a well-earned glass of milk each and some of her home-made cakes.

'How is the vixen?' Gran said.

Mandy smiled. 'Much better,' she said. 'Even her coat is looking redder and glossier. She's getting a lot more rest now that she doesn't have Lucky to look after.'

Gran frowned. 'She won't forget about him, will she?'

Mandy shook her head. 'Oh, no. Dad says as soon as she's well enough she'll be as good a mother as any.'

'That cupboard is quite a favourite of Lucky's,' Grandad said as he unhooked yet another pair of curtains for cleaning.

Gran looked at Lucky, snoozing on the bottom shelf of the old wooden cupboard. 'It's being collected for the auction later today,' she said. 'He'll have to find a new place to sleep.'

'We're going down tonight to help sort the stuff out ready for tomorrow,' Mandy said. 'It's amazing. I think everybody in Welford has donated something.'

'Good way to get rid of your rubbish,' Grandad said and winked.

Mandy laughed. 'It's called recycling, Grandad,' she said. 'It's very green.'

'It might be called recycling,' Grandad said, 'but I'm going to keep a close eye on your gran. There's no telling what she might bring home if the bidding bug bites.'

James looked up and grinned. 'Mrs Ponsonby's pedal-organ?' he said.

Gran laughed. 'I wouldn't have room for it. It would take up the whole of our cottage!'

Mandy looked round her grand-parents' cottage. Even topsyturvy as it was at the moment she loved it. It was just right for them.

'You've got enough room for the two of you and a garden and a greenhouse and friends all around,' she said. 'You wouldn't want to live in a place like

Bleakfell Hall, would you?'

Gran laughed. 'I certainly wouldn't want to spring-clean it!' she said. 'Now, back to work!'

*   *   *

The village hall was crowded when Mandy and James got there that evening. Mr Hope brought them in the Land-rover, with a load of stuff in the back.

'Are you sure you want to give this to the auction, Mandy?' he said as he lifted down a doll's-house that Mandy had had since she was a little girl.

'It's for a good cause,' said Mandy as she looked at it. She was too old to play with a doll's-house any more, but she would still miss it. Her father had made it for her and she had always loved it. The house stood half a metre high. All the doors and windows opened and the back could be removed to reveal the rooms. When she was younger, Mandy had collected lots of furniture for it. Not just tables and chairs and beds, but tiny plates and cups and even small lifelike figures to make a family.

However, everybody else seemed to be giving something. Her mother had donated a beautiful, old china tea-set and James had two bundles of his favourite comics.

Dad lifted down a box of assorted gardening tools and a bundle of golf clubs that he was donating. 'Right,' he said. 'Let's get this stuff inside.'

James pushed the door of the village hall open and Mandy drew in her breath at the sight.

It's like Aladdin's cave!' she said. 'Look at all this!'

The village hall was crammed to bursting. There were tables and chairs and toys and books and mirrors. And, in pride of place down at the front of the auctioneer's table, Mandy saw Mrs Ponsonby's pedal-organ, its wood gleaming with years of polishing. There were even a couple of candle-holders on the front of the case.

'And there's Gran's cupboard and her three-piece suite,' she said, pointing to where the cupboard was wedged in behind a hatstand and a bookcase. Gran had given the suite a good brushing. Mandy looked at the cabbage rose pattern. She would miss that too.

'Who's the auctioneer?' James said.

Mr Hope smiled. 'Walter Pickard,' he said. 'He used to go to cattle auctions when he was a butcher so he knows about these things—or so he says.'

Mandy laughed. 'So long as he doesn't donate a cow or two we'll be all right,' she said. 'I suppose we'd better get started.'

'What do we have to do?' said James.

'First we have to divide things up into lots,' said Adam Hope. He smiled as he saw their faces. 'Bigger items are auctioned on their own. Smaller things are put together.'

'To make lots,' said James. 'Lots of smaller things—that makes sense.'

Mr Hope ran a hand through his hair. 'It isn't quite like that,' he said. 'When you sell something at auction it's called a lot.'

'Even if it's only one thing?' said

Mandy.

Mr Hope smiled. 'Confusing, isn't it?' he said.

Mandy grinned. 'Just you tell us what to do and we'll do it,' she said.

Mr Hope nodded. 'Basically you stick a label with a number on each lot and they're auctioned in that order.'

'Oh, is that all?' said James. 'We can do that,' and he grinned at Mandy.

'If it moves give it something to do,' Walter Pickard said, looking at the Cub Scouts bouncing on the springs of an ancient bed. 'If it doesn't move, label it.'

Mandy and James labelled while Mr Walters, the vicar, entered the lots in a ledger. Mr Walters was to keep track of who bought what while Walter conducted the auction.

By the time nine o'clock came Mandy felt she had stuck labels on just about everything in the village hall.

'That's it,' said Mandy as she stuck a label on the very last object. It was an enormous, green, glass vase and it was absolutely hideous. 'Who gave that?' she said.

She looked at James and they spoke together. 'Mrs Ponsonby!' they said.

'Don't forget to bring Lucky tomorrow,' Tommy Pickard said. 'He's going to be our mascot, Grandad.'

Walter smiled at his grandson. 'As if you hadn't told me a dozen times before,' he said.

'Just don't stick a label on him,' Mandy said. 'We don't want to auction him off.'

Tommy grinned.

'Now, now,' said Mr Walters, bustling up. 'Time to go. You youngsters should be getting off home.' He gathered up the Cubs and shooed them out of the door. He paused as he turned to put the lights off in the hall.

'It's looking very nice,' he said.

Mandy took a last look round the village hall. It still looked like Aladdin's cave but now all the treasures were labelled and entered into Mr Walters' ledger. 'It looks great!' she said. 'I'm sure it's going to be a real success!'

*   *   *

The auction started with an opening ceremony. Mrs Ponsonby, Mr Walters and Walter Pickard were seated on the stage. The vicar and Walter looked a bit uncomfortable but Mrs Ponsonby was in her element.

She stood up, looking as pink as her flowery hat, and called the assembled crowd to order.

'Now,' she said, fixing them with her eyes. 'I want you all to dig deep into your pockets and remember what a good cause you are supporting. The Welford Cub Scouts are depending on you. We've all tried very hard to make this event a success.' She drew herself up. 'I myself have donated some things that are very dear to my heart,' and she looked fondly at the pedal-organ. 'And I hope that you have too,' she went on, her voice severe.

Mandy felt very glad she had given the doll's-house. Even so, it hardly seemed enough when Mrs Ponsonby looked at you like that.

'I only gave some comics,' James whispered.

'But it was your collection,' Mandy said. 'You've been saving them for years.'

'And so,' Mrs Ponsonby was saying, 'without more ado . . .'

There was a cough from behind her and the vicar tried to say something. He looked nervous.

Mrs Ponsonby turned majestically towards him. 'What?' she said.

Mr Walters coughed again. 'I think Mr Pickard would like to say a few words,' he said.

Mrs Ponsonby looked down her nose at Walter Pickard. 'Mr Pickard will be talking all afternoon,' she said. 'He is, after all, conducting the auction.' And she turned back to the hall and said. 'I declare the auction open!'

Mandy spluttered with laughter as she saw Walter Pickard's face.

'I hope he didn't want to say anything important,' said James.

Too bad if he did,' said Mandy. 'With Mrs Ponsonby on her high horse, nobody stands a chance!'

Half an hour later, the auction was going great guns and the lots were falling under the hammer like nine-pins. It really did look as if the day was a runaway success.

Adam Hope was doing afternoon surgery at Animal Ark so he wouldn't be able to get down until late in the afternoon. However, Emily Hope stopped by on her way to Walton and went off loaded with old books and photographs. James's mother and father got an old stone sundial for the garden and Jean Knox bought a big bag of assorted knitting wool. Mandy had a feeling she was going to get a very colourful scarf for Christmas.

Gran and Grandad had dropped in for a while but they couldn't stay too long. The new three-piece suite was being delivered.

'I still like the old one,' Mandy said.

Gran twinkled at her. 'Just you wait till you see the new one,' she said. 'You'll love it!'

Grandad was busy bidding for a stack of flowerpots and a pair of secateurs he thought he could sharpen up.

'Look at that,' said Gran. 'And I'm

supposed to be the one that can't resist an auction!'

Mandy laughed. 'What have you bought?' she said.

Gran brought a beautiful little china figure of a fox cub out of her bag. 'For my new china cabinet,' she said. 'It'll remind me of Lucky.' She looked round. 'Where is he?'

Mandy pointed to the little fox cub, tethered to the leg of a nearby chair. He sat there, playing with his blanket. 'He certainly seems to be bringing the Cubs luck,' she said.

'I think everybody is terrified of Mrs Ponsonby,' said Gran. 'Mrs MacFarlane has just bought a set of six microwave cookery books.'

'What's wrong with that?' said Mandy.

'She hasn't got as a microwave!' said Gran and went off chuckling.

'Lucky and Blackie are getting on well,' said James, watching Gran trying to hurry Grandad along.

Mandy looked down. Lucky was curled up under her chair while Blackie sat proudly in the aisle beside him.

Blackie looks as if he's standing guard over Lucky,' she said.

'He thinks he's a puppy,' said James. Then he smiled. 'Look what's next!' he said.

Mandy looked. It was her doll's-house. She held her breath as she saw Walter hold it up for everyone to see. She almost blushed with pride as he described it. But she had to admit it was a lovely doll's-house.

The bids came thick and fast. Mandy could hardly believe her ears as the price went up and up.

'Your doll's-house is going to pay for a tent all by itself,' said James.

Mandy listened to the bidding. There were only two would-be buyers left in it now.

She looked round and caught the eye of a little girl. It was Penny Hapwell from Twyford Farm. Penny looked at Mandy. Her eyes were shining with excitement. Her father was sitting beside her—and he was bidding for the doll's-house. Mandy found herself hoping that the doll's-house would go to Penny. She had often played with it when she brought Cally, her kitten, to Animal Ark. She truly loved that doll's-house.

'Who else is bidding?' said Mandy.

James looked around. 'There's a man in the corner,' he said. 'But I don't recognise him.'

Mandy twisted round. A dark-haired man in a suit was bidding for her doll's-house.

'That's a dealer,' said a voice in her ear. It was Jean Knox. Mandy hadn't realised she was sitting behind them.

'A dealer?' said Mandy.

'He'll buy it and sell it at a fancy price in London, no doubt,' Jean said.

'In a shop?' said Mandy.

Jean nodded. 'More than likely,' she said. 'People collect things like that.'

Mandy's heart sank. 'But I don't want that,' she said. 'I want another little girl to have it—to play with it. I don't want somebody putting it in a collection.'

The bidding stopped. Mandy hadn't been paying attention. She had been too caught up in what Jean had been saying.

'Going . . .' said Walter, 'going . . . gone!'

Mandy held her breath. Who had bought it—the dealer or Penny's dad?

'To Tom Hapwell of Twyford Farm,' Walter said and Mandy felt the smile spreading across her face.

She turned to look at Penny just as the little girl looked across. Penny had a smile as wide as Mandy's own.

James dug her in the ribs.

'Lot thirty-six,' Walter was saying. 'A fine old pedal-organ. Mahogany casing.' He lifted the lid and peered at the organ. 'Two keyboards. And,' he said, hesitating, 'lots of knobs.'

'Knobs!' said a voice. 'They're called stops.' It was Mrs Ponsonby.

'Does it work?' said a voice from the back of the hall.

'Of course it works!' said Mrs Ponsonby.

Mandy turned round. Mrs Ponsonby was talking to Ernie Bell. Mandy wondered if she had been asking him to make a mantrap for Sam Western.

'How do we know?' said the voice again. Mandy twisted round in her seat

121

to see who it was. Mr Hardy, the owner of the Fox and Goose. Mandy grinned. Mr Hardy knew full well who the organ belonged to. He and Mrs Ponsonby didn't get on. Mrs Ponsonby thought a pub was bad for the village.

'Prove it!' Mr Hardy shouted. His eyes were twinkling with mischief.

Mrs Ponsonby rose to her full height and sailed down the hall towards the organ. 'Are you thinking of starting hymn singing at the pub, Mr Hardy?' she said icily.

Mr Hardy grinned good naturedly. 'I was thinking more of music hall tunes, Mrs Ponsonby. If it works, of course.'

Mrs Ponsonby gave him another icy look, lifted a chair as she passed Mandy and plonked it down in front of the organ.

She pedalled briskly, working up a good head of air, then launched into 'Rock of Ages'. The room resounded to the notes pouring out of the instrument. It didn't only work—it was amazing! Mandy could feel her ears ringing.

Then Mrs Ponsonby started to sing.

It was awful. The organ was playing the tune all right. But Mrs Ponsonby seemed to be singing something completely different.

'Ouch!' said James, clamping his hands to his ears.

Blackie set up a howl and a couple of other dogs joined in. With the organ and Mrs Ponsonby and the dogs, the noise was deafening. Only Pandora and

Toby seemed to be unaffected by Mrs Ponsonby's singing. Maybe they were used to it, Mandy thought.

There was a scraping of chairs as several people suddenly found they had to leave in a hurry.

'All right, all right. I believe you!' came a shout from the back of the room. But Mrs Ponsonby either didn't hear or refused to take any notice.

Eventually she brought the hymn to a close with a resounding crash of chords and turned triumphantly to Mr Hardy, who had his fingers in his ears.

'Is that proof enough?' she said. 'Or would you like another demonstration—before you buy it?'

Mr Hardy looked resigned. All around him people were trying to hide their amusement. Some weren't bothering to hide it.

'I reckon you got your comeuppance there all right, Bob,' said Ernie Bell, chuckling.

Mr Hardy grinned back. 'I reckon I did, Ernie,' he said. 'So if nobody else is interested I'll give you—'

'There's a minimum price on this lot!' Mrs Ponsonby said majestically. She turned to Walter Pickard, who was enjoying every moment of this. Mandy was almost sure she saw her wink. Mrs Ponsonby? Surely not.

Poor Mr Hardy ended up paying a fortune for the organ.

'It's for a good cause,' Walter said later on. 'He should know better than to tangle with Amelia Ponsonby!'

They were gathering up the unsold items. Just about everybody had left.

Mandy grinned and stretched. She was tired. But the auction had been a great success. There was still a lot of stuff lying around waiting to be collected, but most people had taken their purchases with them.

'Come on, James,' she said. 'Let's get Lucky back to Ernie's.'

She looked down, expecting to see Lucky still curled up with his blanket, tethered to the chair. The lead was still there but it hung slackly. Lucky wasn't under the chair. He wasn't anywhere. Lucky had gone!

CHAPTER EIGHT

'Where can he have gone?' said Mandy. 'Where is he?'

'He was there all afternoon,' said James, looking at the floor beside Mandy.

Mandy looked round frantically. Nearly everybody had gone. Mrs Ponsonby was still talking to Ernie Bell over by the door. Walter Pickard was starting to clear up and Mr Walters was adding up the figures in his ledger at the auction table. But there was no sign of the little fox cub.

Mr Walters looked up from his ledger. 'We've had a very good day,' he said, beaming at them all. 'I think we'll manage some other camping equipment as well as the tents.'

But Mandy wasn't listening. Her mind was still on Lucky. 'He must be somewhere,' she said. 'Oh, James, if he gets out of the hall he could wander off anywhere! You know how adventurous he is. Anything could happen to him. He could get run over. He could have an accident.' Her eyes opened wide. 'What if there are more of those awful traps around? What if he gets caught in one? We've got to find him!'

'What's all this then?' said Walter Pickard. 'What's the problem?'

Mandy told him swiftly. 'He was here,' she said pointing to the lead still attached to the chair leg beside her.

'We'll look for him,' said Walter. 'Just stay calm and let's do this in an organised way. After all, we can't go losing the Cubs' mascot.'

'Oh,' said Mandy. 'Tommy will be so upset!'

Walter shook his head. 'He will that,' he said. 'He's gone to deliver a couple of things to the MacFarlanes. Let's see if we can find Lucky before he gets back.'

Walter got them organised. They fanned out into a line covering every bit of the hall, looking in boxes and under chairs and even inside the enormous green vase. But there was no sign of Lucky.

'Perhaps he got out of the hall,' Mandy said at last. 'What if we never find him?'

'Now, now,' said Walter, 'don't give up yet, young miss. There are other places to look.'

So they looked under the small stage at the end of the hall and behind the stairwell and in the loos. Mr Hope came back from his afternoon surgery as they were giving up hope of finding Lucky.

'Oh, Dad, he's lost,' Mandy said. 'What if he gets into one of those traps?'

'Hmmph,' said Mrs Ponsonby. 'Just let me get a word with Sam Western and I'll tell him what he can do with those traps!'

Just then the phone rang. Mandy turned hopefully towards the sound. Mr Walters hurried over and picked up the receiver. 'For you,' he said to Adam Hope.

Mandy's father went to take the call while Mandy breathed a sigh. It wasn't news of Lucky then.

'What's the matter?' said a voice from the doorway.

Mandy looked round. It was Tommy. She hesitated. She didn't want to upset him. But he was already looking round the hall.

'Where's Lucky?' he said. 'Where's our mascot? He really was lucky for us, wasn't he, Grandad? Have we made enough money to buy our tents now? Can we go camping this summer?'

Walter looked down at his grandson. 'More than enough,' he said. 'You'll have your summer camp this year.'

'Oh, good!' said Tommy but his eyes were still searching the hall. 'Where's Lucky?' he said again. 'I want to tell him he brought us good luck.'

Walter cleared his throat. 'Lucky has gone and got himself lost,' he said. 'Silly little cub. But he'll turn up, don't you worry.'

Tommy looked puzzled. 'Lost?' he

said. Then his face brightened up. 'Oh, I bet he's still in the cupboard. I didn't think he would sleep this long.'

Six faces turned to the little boy—Mandy, James, Mr Hope, Mrs Ponsonby, Walter and Ernie.

'*What?*' they all said at once.

Tommy took a step backwards and looked unsure of himself. 'He was so sleepy,' he said. 'And when Mrs Ponsonby started to play the organ he didn't like the noise. So I unclipped him and put him in the cupboard with his blanket. He likes it in there.'

'Cupboard?' said Walter. 'What cupboard?'

'I think I know,' said Mandy. 'It was Gran's china cupboard, wasn't it, Tommy?'

Tommy nodded. He was beginning to look a little frightened. 'I didn't do anything wrong,' he said. 'It's Lucky's cupboard.'

James smiled down at him. 'That's all right, Tommy,' he said. 'He's probably still there.'

Tommy nodded proudly. 'Oh, he will be,' he said. 'I made sure the door was closed.'

Mandy's breath stopped in her throat and then she remembered that the cupboard had a lattice-work front. At least Lucky would have plenty of air. Then a thought struck her. 'Where is it?' she said to James. 'I didn't see it when we were looking.'

They made a quick tour of all the furniture that was left but the cupboard wasn't there. It had gone.

'But where?' said James.

'What if that dealer bought it?' Mandy said. 'What if he's taken it to London?'

Mr Walters looked up from his ledger. 'We'll soon find out,' he said. 'It's all here in my ledger.'

He took out a pair of half-moon glasses and put them carefully on his nose. Mandy was almost dancing with impatience but she knew there was no point in hurrying him.

James couldn't bear it. He watched Mr Walters' bony finger travel slowly down the length of the list of objects and buyers.

'Let me look,' James said, his own

glasses nearly tipping off the end of his nose.

Mr Walters tutted and frowned. 'Now I'll have to start again,' he said. 'You young people have got no patience.'

James looked at Mandy in anguish as the vicar started at the beginning again, finger following the lot numbers down the page, turning each page of the ledger carefully, adjusting his glasses.

At last after what seemed an eternity he said, 'Here it is. Lot number forty-two.'

'Who bought it?' said Mandy.

'Just let me look,' said Mr Walters.

He peered at the page and adjusted his glasses again. 'Ah, the Spry sisters,' he said at last. 'And they took it with them to The Riddings, it says here,' he peered. 'Ernie was doing this bit and I can't read his writing.' Ernie Bell started to say something but Mr Walters went on. 'Oh, yes. Collected by Sam Western,' he said.

'Mr Western?' said Mandy. 'What was he doing here?' Sam Western was much too grand to come to a Cub

132

Scout auction.

'He wanted to talk to the Sprys,' said Ernie. 'He took them home in that posh car of his. I remember now they had some sort of cupboard in the back.'

Mandy and James looked at each other, horrified. One awful thought followed another. It wasn't hard to guess what Mr Western wanted to talk to the Sprys about—the fox-hunting. And poor little Lucky was locked in a cupboard in his car!

'We've got to get him back!' said James.

Mandy nodded. 'And quickly,' she said. She turned to look for her dad.

Adam Hope was striding across the hall in a purposeful way. He stopped as he passed them. 'Look, Mandy,' he said, 'I won't be back for an hour or so. There's a suspected outbreak of staggers at Baildon Farm and I said I'd go up there at once.'

Mandy bit her lip. She had hoped he would be able to take them to The Riddings. 'OK, Dad,' she said.

'I could ring home,' said James as Mr Hope hurried out of the door.

Mandy shook her head. 'We can't waste time waiting,' she said. 'We've got to go there—at once! We've got to get Lucky back!'

'The bikes are outside,' James said. 'How long ago did the Sprys leave?'

Ernie looked doubtful. 'Not more than half an hour,' he said.

'Half an hour?' said Mandy.

James looked at her. 'Time enough for the Sprys to have opened that cupboard,' he said.

'We have to go like the wind,' said Mandy. 'We can't take Blackie. He'll never keep up.'

James turned to Blackie. 'Stay,' he said sternly. Blackie looked up at him and wagged his tail. 'Stay!' said James again even more shortly and the Labrador looked puzzled.

'Come on, James!' said Mandy.

James turned and followed her, leaving Blackie looking sad and lonely. 'Just think of the scare the Sprys will get when they find Lucky,' he said as they made their way out of the hall. 'They'll probably faint with fright.'

'There's an even worse thought,'

Mandy said as they got on their bikes and headed off for The Riddings.

'What could be worse?' said James.

Mandy turned a serious face towards him. 'What if Mr Western finds Lucky first?' she said.

CHAPTER NINE

James's straight, brown hair blew back from his forehead as they hurtled past the crossroads at the Fox and Goose and turned on to the Walton Road.

As they passed the pub they could see Mr Hardy standing in front of the pedal organ which was sitting in front of the pub. It looked as if he couldn't get it through the door. He gave them a cheery wave as they passed but Mandy and James had no time to stop. They had to get to The Riddings as fast as possible.

'I wish your dad hadn't had to go out on that call,' said James. 'He could have stood up to Mr Western.'

Mandy's face set. 'He had to go,' she

said. 'The staggers can be really serious for cattle. We'll just have to stand up to Mr Western on our own.'

James was breathing heavily as they pedalled up the hill out of Welford.

'What do you think Mr Western will do if he finds Lucky?' he panted.

Mandy gave him a brief look before shooting round the corner at the top of the hill. 'I don't even want to think about it, James!' she called back as she whizzed down the hill.

Pedalling was easier now and in the distance she could see the chimneys of The Riddings rising above the trees. Only a mile to go.

'Oh, please, please, let us be in time,' she muttered to herself. 'Please!'

*   *   *

They left the bikes at the side of the steps and looked up at the massive front door.

'He's still here,' James said pointing to Mr Western's car.

Mandy looked through the car windows. 'No cupboard, though,' she said.

'They must have taken it inside,' said James. 'Unless it's in the boot.'

Mandy bit her lip. 'We'd better look,' she said.

James hesitated. 'It might be locked,' he said.

Mandy thought of poor Lucky locked in a cupboard in the boot of a car. They'd have to take their chances.

'There's only one way to find out,' she said. 'If he's still in there we've got to get him out!'

James pushed his glasses up his nose and took a deep breath. 'OK,' he said. 'You keep a lookout. I'll open the boot.'

Mandy fixed her eyes on the windows at the front of the house. The place seemed deserted, except for Mr Western's car. But The Riddings was so enormous. Mr Western and the Spry sisters could be anywhere.

'It isn't locked,' said James and Mandy turned to him.

'Is he there?' she said eagerly.

James was looking down into the car boot as if turned to stone. Mandy's heart started hammering against her chest.

'What is it, James?' she said. 'What have you found? Is it Lucky? Is he—' She couldn't bear to say it. 'Is he hurt?' she said at last.

James shook his head. 'No,' he said. 'It isn't Lucky. He isn't here and neither is the cupboard.'

'So what *is* there?' said Mandy, puzzled. She couldn't understand what was making James look like that.

James turned to her. 'See for yourself,' he said.

Mandy came and looked into the boot. For a moment she could hardly speak. 'Traps!' she said. 'More of those horrible traps!'

James turned to her. 'Lucky must be inside,' he said. 'They must have taken the cupboard into the house. I just hope he's still in the cupboard. We've got to get him before Mr Western does!'

Mandy dragged her eyes away from the evil-looking traps. As she did so she thought she caught a movement behind the curtains of the drawing-room window. But she was too worried to pay any attention. 'Right,' she said. 'Let's go!'

'What? We just march up and knock on the door?' said James.

'Why not?' said Mandy. 'Who's going to stop us?'

Just at that moment the front door flew open. 'What are you doing to my car?' said Sam Western, his face red with fury. James shut the boot lid with a crash.

'We want to see Miss Marjorie!'

'Or Miss Joan!' said James.

Mr Western stood at the top of the steps looking down at them. He put his hands on his hips. He looked huge standing up there. 'So you think you'll find them in the boot of my car?' he said.

Mandy opened her mouth to speak but he cut her short. 'I know you two,' he said. 'You're the two young troublemakers from Welford, aren't you? I might have known.'

'We aren't troublemakers,' Mandy began, then she saw a small figure appear behind Mr Western. 'Oh, Miss

Joan, we need to talk to you.'

'Make yourselves scarce,' Mr Western said. 'Go on, get out of it before I call the police!' He turned to Miss Joan. 'I've just caught these two in the boot of my car,' he said. 'Up to no good, I'll be bound.'

Mandy bit her lip. 'But we weren't ...' she began. At that moment Blackie appeared. Patch began to squirm in Miss Joan's arms as Blackie started barking.

'Oh, Blackie!' said James. 'I told you to stay!' He bent down and gave the Labrador a pat. Blackie looked up at him adoringly and wagged his tail.

'And get that animal out of here as well,' Mr Western said. 'Can't you see he's upsetting Miss Spry's cat?' He turned to Miss Joan and ushered her back into the house. 'Young ruffians,' he said to her. 'Don't you worry. They won't get across the doorstep!'

Miss Joan looked worriedly at Blackie. 'Oh, dear,' she said. 'Patch is so timid. Maybe it would be better if you came back another day, dears. Without your dog.'

'But, Miss Joan!' Mandy began again.

But Mr Western gave them a final look and almost pushed Miss Joan back into the house. 'I want to talk to you about these two,' he said and slammed the door.

James ran a hand through his hair. 'Well,' he said. 'That's that. What on earth are we going to do now?'

Mandy's mouth set. 'We're going to get Lucky out of that cupboard. That's what we're going to do!' she said.

James looked at her. 'You heard Miss Joan,' he said. 'She won't let us in. Not with Blackie here anyway.' He bent down and patted the Labrador. 'Sorry, Blackie. And if we knock on the door again Mr Western will call the police.'

Mandy's eyes sparked fire. 'Maybe that wouldn't be a bad idea,' she said. 'Considering what he's got in the boot of his car. But we don't have time to waste. We've got to get to Lucky as soon as possible. He must still be in the cupboard. The sisters can't know anything about him yet—nor can Sam

Western.'

'But they still won't let us in,' said James.

Mandy sighed. 'So, if they won't let us in, we'll have to find another way.'

'What way?' said James.

Mandy frowned, then looked at him very seriously. 'James,' she said. 'I think we're going to have to sneak in.'

James gasped. 'Sneak in?' he said.

Mandy nodded. 'Can you think of any other way of getting in there?'

James shook his head slowly.

'And we *do* have to get into the house,' said Mandy.

James nodded. 'If there's nothing else for it, I suppose we'll have to,' he said.

Mandy looked worried. 'There isn't anything else for it,' she said. 'But first we have to look as if we're doing what we were told to do and go away.' She cast a quick glance over her shoulder and saw a curtain twitch at the drawing room window. 'Come on,' she said.

'Where?' said James.

'We'll ride down the drive and out of the gates. Then we'll hide the bikes and creep back in through the trees. We can get round to the back of the house without anybody seeing us if we're careful.'

James grinned. 'Mr Western will go mad if he catches us,' he said.

'Then we'll have to make sure he doesn't catch us,' Mandy said. 'Come on. What are you waiting for?'

*   *   *

They hid the bikes among the bushes at the end of the drive and tethered Blackie by his lead to a tree.

'Sorry, Blackie,' James said. 'But we can't have you barking and giving the game away.'

Blackie licked his face happily. He didn't mind. He seemed to think this was a new kind of game.

'You can guard the bikes, Blackie,' said Mandy. 'That's an important job.' She gave the Labrador a pat.

Getting through the trees wasn't all that easy. They grew thickly almost up to the house but provided good cover. They couldn't risk being out in the open. They could see Geoffrey, the gardener, on the far side of the lawn.

'He's weeding,' said James.

'Let's just hope he doesn't turn round as we cross the open space to the house,' Mandy said. She didn't fancy having to explain herself to Geoffrey.

At last they were round the corner of the house. They could see the back door from the shelter of the trees.

'Suppose someone is watching out of a window,' James said.

'We'll have to risk it,' Mandy said. 'Anyway, Mr Western will be in the drawing-room with the Sprys. He thinks we've gone. They won't be looking out of the windows round here.'

'OK,' said James. 'Let's go then!'

They crossed the short open space to the back door quickly but quietly, and sheltered under the portico over the door.

'We've done it!' said Mandy. Then she saw James's face. 'What is it?'

'The back door is locked,' he said miserably.

Mandy sighed. 'How are we going to

get in?'

Carefully, trying to make as little noise as possible, they made their way round the house. They tried window after window but all were locked. Mandy was almost in despair when she looked up. There, above her head was a small window—and it was open.

'Look!' she said, pointing.

'We'll never get through that,' said James.

'Oh, yes, we will,' said Mandy determinedly. 'It's our only chance.'

James looked doubtful but Mandy was determined to try.

'I'll go first,' she said. 'Can you give me a leg up?'

'OK,' said James. 'Tell me when you're ready and I'll give you an extra boost.'

James cupped his hands and Mandy put her foot firmly on them and hoisted herself up. Her fingers grasped the window ledge.

'Now!' she said, and James shoved with all his strength.

Mandy's fingers gripped hard on the ledge, then she got a foothold in a crack in the wall and she was there, perched on the ledge.

Quickly she thrust one leg over the sill and scrambled through the window. The drop on the other side was bigger than she thought it would be and she landed heavily. 'Ouch,' she said as she hit the floor.

'You all right?' came James's voice from outside.

'Fine,' said Mandy getting up. She could just see the top of James's head over the window ledge. 'Wait, I'll get a chair or something, then I can climb up and haul you up.'

'What room are you in?' James whispered.

Mandy looked round. 'I don't think it's a room at all,' she said. She looked at the jars and bottles and packages on shelves round the walls. 'It looks like a big old-fashioned larder,' she said.

Carefully she opened the door to the room outside—and breathed a sigh of relief. There was nobody there.

She dragged a chair over to the window and scrambled up on it. 'All clear,' she called.

She stretched out her arms and James grasped them round the wrists, climbing with his feet up the wall below the window. With a heave she pulled him through the window and he landed in a heap on top of her when the chair fell over.

'Shh!' said Mandy as James grunted.

'I don't think we'd make very good burglars,' said James.

'Maybe not,' said Mandy, 'but we're the best we've got. Now we've got to look for that cupboard.'

'We'll have to hurry,' said James. 'But quietly.'

On tiptoe they searched downstairs. One by one they opened doors. They found huge, almost empty rooms draped in faded curtains. They tried the last room on the passageway between the dining-room and the hall.

Mandy beckoned to James. 'In here,' she said.

James came and stood beside her. There, in the middle of the huge room was Gran's little china cupboard.

'Listen,' said Mandy. They could hear a very faint whining sound. 'Lucky!' she said. 'He's there after all!'

She ran to the cupboard, tugging at the door handle until the door opened and Lucky almost fell out in his eagerness at hearing her voice. He began to give sharp little yelps.

'Shh!' said James as Lucky tumbled over himself to get into Mandy's arms. Mandy was hugging him, her face wreathed in smiles.

'Oh, Lucky,' she said. 'It's good to see you!'

Lucky's yelps got louder.

'Hush!' Mandy said to him. 'Somebody will hear you!'

But the little animal was too excited to stop.

Mandy picked up Lucky's blanket. There was a sound in the hall and suddenly the door opened. Mr Western stood there with the Spry sisters behind him.

'What's going on here?' he thundered. Then he saw what Mandy was holding.

Mandy shrank back in fear. Not of Mr Western. She wasn't afraid of him. But beside him were his two bulldogs. They were advancing with teeth bared towards the fox cub in her arms.

CHAPTER TEN

'Drop it!' shouted Sam Western as the dogs advanced on Mandy. 'Drop the cub!'

Mandy looked at him, her mouth set grimly. In front of her the dogs padded across the room from the door, nostrils twitching, scenting the frightened little cub. Then one of them drew back its lips from its teeth and snarled.

'Drop it!' shouted Sam Western again. 'They'll get you as well if you don't!'

The sisters appeared in the doorway.

'Oh, please, do as he says,' Miss Joan said. Mandy looked at her, standing there with Patch in her arms. The cat was trembling with fright.

Then she looked at the dogs and swallowed hard. 'No!' she said. 'Call them off.'

'I can't call them off!' Sam Western shouted. 'They've got the scent of that fox.' Then he realised Mandy was serious and leaped for his dogs but he was too slow. 'For goodness sake, girl, drop that cub!' he shouted as he tried to reach the dogs.

'No,' said Mandy again.

The dogs were closer now. She saw one of them swing his big head to the side and sniff. Patch quivered in Miss Joan's arms and let out a piteous miaow.

Then the dog gathered himself on his haunches—ready to leap for the poor, defenceless, little cub. Sam Western made a final lunge for the dogs and the two animals sprang.

'Mandy!' James called in terror.

Mandy closed her eyes and held on to Lucky. There was a sudden yowl— and a scream from Miss Joan.

Mandy's eyes flew open in time to see Patch land on the floor. He must have leaped out of Miss Joan's arms.

Confused, the little cat ran for cover. But he ran across the path of the dogs. Miss Joan flung herself forward to save her pet. Miss Marjorie grasped her sister's sleeve.

The dogs turned and snarled. They lost interest in the cub and began to chase Patch. But Patch was too quick for them. He gave a heart-stopping screech and raced for the curtains. He scampered up the fraying, dusty material, clinging with his claws. Halfway up, he turned and spat at the dogs.

The dogs bayed and howled at the little cat, jumping at the curtains, tearing them.

Mandy shoved Lucky back into the cupboard.

'Sorry,' she said to the little cub. 'But with these two on the loose this is the safest place for you!'

Mr Western was calling his dogs but they paid no attention. They were leaping at the curtains now. Dust flew from the ancient material and there was a ripping sound as they gave way.

Patch leaped for safety as the whole

lot came down and covered the dogs. Sam Western ran for his dogs just as Patch jumped. The kitten twisted in the air to avoid him but it was impossible. Patch landed on Sam Western's back and sank his claws into his neck. Sam Western let out a roar. His dogs were still entangled in the curtains. They were snarling at each other now. But they couldn't get free of the curtains.

Mandy heaved a sigh of relief.

'Good for you, Patch!' shouted Miss Joan.

Mandy nearly giggled as she watched—except that she was still shaking with fright.

'Are you all right?' said James.

Mandy nodded. 'Let's just get out of here with Lucky,' she said.

Patch sprang lightly from Sam Western's back and padded across the floor to Miss Joan.

'Clever kitty,' said Miss Marjorie as the little cat stalked out of the room.

Sam Western had untangled his dogs now and was dipping their leads on.

'Those two have got a filthy fox cub in that cupboard!' he roared.

'He is not filthy,' said James. 'We gave him a bath the other day.'

'And as for that animal you call a cat!' Sam Western said, rubbing the back of his neck. 'It ought to be put down.'

'How dare you say that about Patch, Mr Western?' Miss Joan said.

'Mr Western,' said Miss Marjorie, outraged. 'Control yourself!'

Mandy looked round the room. The dogs were growling. Mr Western was mopping the blood on his neck with his handkerchief. The sisters were looking very angry indeed. And James had come to stand beside her and the cupboard.

'Ask what they've got in that cupboard,' said Mr Western. 'Go on ask. Filthy vermin.'

'Mr Western!' said Miss Marjorie.

Mr Western looked furious. 'I mean the fox cub,' he said. 'If you let me use your land for hunting you won't have all this nonsense.'

'You can't!' said Mandy to the Spry sisters. 'You can't let him do it! He's already setting traps for them. Do you remember when we brought the vixen and fox cub here? It was Mr Western that set that trap!'

'And we found another one the other day,' said James. 'We got to it just in time to stop Mrs Ponsonby's peke getting hurt.'

'So it was you who sprang those traps!' said Mr Western, his face black as thunder. 'Just wait till . . .' and he took a few threatening strides towards them.

Miss Marjorie's voice was hard as she said. 'You set traps, Mr Western?'

Sam Western stopped in his tracks.

156

Mandy could see him realise what he had said. 'No, no,' he said. 'My manager may have done—without my knowing—but I know how much you disapprove of traps. Hunting is a very different matter.'

'I'm very glad to hear it,' Miss Joan said.

'Dear Papa always said hunting was for gentlemen but traps were not,' said Miss Marjorie.

'He did set them, or at least he knew about them,' said James.

Sam Western turned to him. 'I'd advise you to keep quiet, young man,' he said. 'Anyone who has broken into a house should say as little as possible.'

Mandy stepped forward. 'It's easy enough to prove,' she said. 'All we have to do is look in the boot of his car. There are more traps there.'

'Nonsense!' said Mr Western, clearly rattled. 'Pack of lies.'

Mandy took a step forward. 'Why don't we let Miss Joan and Miss Marjorie see for themselves?' she said.

'Outrageous,' said Mr Western. 'The cheek of it. I don't have to agree to anything.'

'Perhaps not,' said Miss Joan quietly, 'but it would make us wonder why you are so reluctant to show us what is in the boot of your car.'

Mr Western spluttered but he knew he was beaten. 'I don't know why you're so bothered about them,' he said. 'You set traps to catch vermin and foxes are just vermin.'

'It's because the traps are so cruel, Mr Western,' said Miss Marjorie quietly. 'And I think you are a cruel man. To set those dogs on a child!'

'I didn't,' said Sam Western. 'I told her to drop the cub.'

'As if I would!' said Mandy.

Miss Joan turned to her. 'I think Mandy has shown us what caring for animals is really about,' she said.

'She was ready to defend that little cub to the last,' said Miss Marjorie.

'If she is willing to do something like that,' said Miss Joan, 'how can we allow you to kill foxes on our land?'

'You know, I begin to think that perhaps Father was wrong,' said Miss Marjorie.

Miss Joan looked a little shocked but she supported her sister. 'No matter what we think about fox-hunting,' she said, 'we certainly could not allow you on to our land—not after this, Mr Western. We are all God's creatures, you see, and we really have no right to kill these animals.'

'We can see that now—thanks to Mandy,' said Miss Marjorie.

'So if you would be so good as to go away now,' said Miss Joan.

'And please don't come back,' said Miss Marjorie.

A face suddenly appeared at the window. Geoffrey, the gardener. He looked at the curtains lying inside the room and pushed his cap back on his head.

'Been a bit of a to-do, then?' he said, scratching his head.

'You could say that, Geoffrey,' said Miss Joan.

Geoffrey looked at Sam Western and his dogs. 'Need any help then?' he said.

'Mr Western was just leaving,' said Miss Marjorie with all her dignity.

The gardener put his cap back on his

head. 'Good,' he said. 'Never did like him—or his dogs,' and he stomped off across the lawn.

Mandy saw Mr Western open his mouth to try to speak but he was lost for words.

'Heel!' he said to his dogs and Mandy watched him stride out of the room into the hall and down the steps to his car. She suddenly remembered something and rushed after him.

'If we find any more of these traps,' she shouted, 'we shall know where to send the police.'

Mr Western turned to her. 'Namby-pamby animal lover,' he said. 'Just you stay out of my way in future! I always knew you were a troublemaker!'

Mandy came back into the room to find the sisters cooing over Lucky whom James had released from the cupboard.

'He's as good as new,' said James. 'Being in the cupboard hasn't done him a bit of harm.'

Mandy smiled. 'He always did like that cupboard,' she said.

'Oh, look at him!' said Miss

Marjorie. 'His coat is quite red now.'

'And he still has the blanket we gave him,' said Miss Joan. 'How sweet.'

The twins looked at each other over the cub's furry head. 'How could anybody want to hunt down a sweet little creature like this?' said Miss Joan.

Miss Marjorie shook her head. 'It's positively wicked,' she said. 'Now, who would like a cup of tea?'

Mandy looked at James and smiled. He looked as relieved as she felt. They could relax now. There would be no more traps for animals and no fox hunting in Welford. She looked down at the cub in her arms.

'You *are* Lucky,' she said. 'Lucky for yourself and lucky for all the other little fox cubs you're going to save from being hunted.'

Lucky gave a short bark, his eyes as bright as buttons.

Mandy laughed. 'Come on!' she said to the little creature. 'We'll see if we can get you some bread and milk.'

CHAPTER ELEVEN

After Mr Western had gone Miss Joan turned to Mandy and said, 'We would like it very much if Lucky and his mother could be released on to our land—when the time comes.'

'Yes, indeed,' Miss Marjorie said. 'We feel responsible for them somehow.'

'If it hadn't been for us not standing up to Mr Western none of this would have happened,' said Miss Joan.

'Oh, no,' Mandy said. 'You mustn't think that. You couldn't have stopped him laying those traps.'

'In fact,' James put in, 'if all this hadn't happened we wouldn't have proof that he was the one laying the traps. It was just our word against his. But now he's admitted in front of you that it was him.'

'So you see,' said Mandy, cuddling Lucky, 'it really all worked out for the best. There won't be any more traps now and your land will be safe for foxes.'

'Indeed it will,' said Miss Joan with spirit. 'There will be no hunting on our land.'

'You can rest assured of that!' Miss Marjorie added.

'And I can't think of anywhere I'd rather let them go than here at The Riddings,' said Mandy. 'If it hadn't been for you letting Mum work in your kitchen, Lucky's mother might not have survived at all—and then Lucky wouldn't have survived either.'

The sisters looked pleased.

Then Mandy and James took Lucky back to Ernie Bell's house. Ernie chuckled when they told him how the sisters had stood up to Mr Western.

'And you mark my words,' he said as he put Lucky gently back in his pen,

163

'Sam Western won't dare to lay any more traps now. There are too many of us as know about it for him to go around doing a thing like that again.'

Ernie looked at the little cub scampering about his pen, none the worse for his adventure. 'I'll miss him when he goes,' he said. 'But he's a wild creature and the wild is the place for him.'

'We're going to release him and his mother on the Sprys' land,' said Mandy.

Ernie smiled. 'They'll find good cover there,' he said. 'You let me know when and I'll come with you.'

'Great!' said James. 'We can give them a real send-off!'

Mandy turned to him, her face alight. 'Who else will we invite?' she said.

James grinned. 'Everybody who's been interested in Lucky,' he said.

Mandy shook her head. 'That's nearly the whole village,' she said. 'The Spry sisters are shy, remember.'

James looked thoughtful. 'Not as shy as they used to be,' he said. 'Remember when they first adopted Patch?'

Mandy nodded. Adopting the kitten had made a real difference to the sisters.

'If we gather all the people together who really cared for Lucky and his mother,' James said, 'they won't be shy of them—how could they be?'

Mandy's face brightened. 'I think you're right,' she said. 'Who shall we start with?'

'Your gran and grandad?' said James.

'Let's go and tell them,' said Mandy.

*   *   *

Lilac Cottage was as neat as a new pin when they arrived. All the havoc of spring-cleaning had gone, leaving the cottage in shining apple pie order. Mandy and James gave Gran their news as they tumbled into the cottage with Blackie at their heels.

'You can count on us to be there,' said Gran, 'Now, what do you think of my new three-piece suite?'

Mandy looked round and gasped at

what she saw.

'Gran?' she said, staring at the new three-piece suite.

'I told you you would like it,' said Gran.

'But it's the same as the old one,' Mandy said.

'As near as makes no difference,' said Gran. 'I always liked the old one.'

Mandy looked at the familiar cottage, at the new suite with its pattern of cabbage roses.

'Of course it isn't frayed like the old one—or faded,' said Gran.

Mandy laughed. 'Nothing's changed, Gran,' she said. 'It's all just the same.' And she felt a warm glow. She hadn't wanted Lilac Cottage to change—not the tiniest bit.

'Some things change,' said Gran. 'Your dad says Lucky's mother is coming on a treat now. It won't be long before she's ready to leave Animal Ark.'

Mandy felt a swift pang of sadness. Then she remembered what Ernie Bell had said. He was right—wild creatures belonged in the wild.

And soon it was time to say goodbye to Lucky and his mother. Mr and Mrs Hope had both come to The Riddings. The Sprys had laid on tea and delicious home-made cakes.

The sisters were dressed in their Sunday best. Miss Joan had a large, floppy, straw hat with a bunch of flowers weighing down the brim. Miss Marjorie looked wonderful in a long silk skirt and frilly blouse. Even Geoffrey had turned out for the occasion. He was dressed in his best tweed jacket and a brand-new pair of Wellington boots.

Gran and Grandad were there too, and Ernie Bell and Walter Pickard and Tommy.

They were all gathered outside The Riddings. The Spry sisters were in a flutter of nervousness when Mrs Ponsonby arrived. She got out of her car with Toby and Pandora at her heels. Blackie immediately went over to play with them.

'Oh, no,' James muttered to Mandy. 'I hope he behaves!'

'Call him,' said Mandy.

James looked at her. 'And show Mrs Ponsonby how disobedient he is?' he said. 'She would have Blackie signed up for those obedience classes in no time!'

Mrs Ponsonby came towards them like a ship in full sail. 'I just came to tell you, Miss Joan and Miss Marjorie,' she said, 'that I have spoken most severely to Mr Western. I explained that he is not under any circumstances to bother you again with this nonsense about fox-hunting!'

The Spry sisters fluttered even more. 'That was very kind of you, Mrs Ponsonby,' said Miss Joan.

Mrs Ponsonby drew herself up. 'Not at all,' she said. 'The man had to be taught a lesson. And let me tell you that the whole of Welford admires you for standing up to him.'

Miss Joan and Miss Marjorie went quite pink at the compliment. Then Ernie Bell broke in.

'Maybe you should get Sam Western

along to those obedience classes of yours at the village hall,' he said and chuckled.

Mrs Ponsonby looked down her nose at him. 'I have decided,' she said, 'that I will not be running the obedience classes after all.'

Mandy heard James gasp.

'Why would that be, Mrs Ponsonby?' Mr Hope said, with a twinkle in his eye, 'I thought you were a great believer in training animals.'

Emily Hope nudged her husband. 'Don't tease,' she said.

But Mrs Ponsonby was speaking again. 'If you must know, it was these two who changed my mind,' she said, looking at Mandy and James.

'Us?' said Mandy, feeling puzzled.

'Certainly,' said Mrs Ponsonby. 'If Toby had come when he was called then Pandora would have gone to investigate that trap. It was Toby being disobedient that saved my precious Pandora.' She looked at where Toby and Pandora were rolling in a patch of mud with Blackie.

Mandy saw her open her mouth to

call the dogs, then close it again. 'Obedience isn't everything,' Mrs Ponsonby said firmly.

'No obedience classes?' said James. He sounded as if he could hardly believe it.

Mrs Ponsonby gave him a look. Then she turned towards Blackie, who was digging a hole in a flower-bed and encouraging Toby and Pandora to do the same.

Geoffrey saw them too. 'Get out of there!' he shouted.

'Of course I could make an exception for Blackie,' Mrs Ponsonby said.

'Oh, no!' said James. 'Don't. I mean, don't bother, don't trouble yourself.' He sprinted over to get hold of Blackie and drag him back.

Mrs Ponsonby turned to Mandy and this time there was no mistake. She definitely *did* wink. Mandy giggled.

'Time to let these two go,' said Adam Hope as he lifted two cages out of the back of the Land-rover.

Mandy's giggles stopped abruptly. Now she would have to say goodbye to

Lucky and his mother.

'I think you two should do it,' said Mrs Hope to Mandy and James.

Ernie Bell took hold of Blackie's collar and Adam Hope gave the cage with the vixen in it to James. Then he bent and picked up the cage with Lucky in it. 'This is your job, Mandy,' he said.

Mandy looked at the little fox cub. He had grown so much in the last weeks. His coat was russet, his ears pricked and alert and his eyes were bright and intelligent as he looked at her. She swallowed. She couldn't speak.

'Let them go in amongst the trees,' said Ernie Bell. 'They'll be more at home there. And it'll be quieter. Not so many people around.'

Mandy looked at him gratefully. He understood that she wanted to be by herself when she let Lucky go.

'You go ahead,' said Gran. 'I want to talk to Miss Marjorie and Miss Joan about these delicious cakes.'

'If you want the recipe, we'd be only too glad,' said Miss Marjorie.

171

Gran looked at the sisters. 'Oh, I couldn't make them as well as you do,' she said. 'No, I was wondering if you would help out at my baked goods stall at the church bazaar next month—and bake some cakes for it, of course.'

'Us?' said Miss Joan. 'Oh, we've never done anything like that before.'

Grandad smiled. 'There's nothing to it,' he said. 'And, besides, you'd be among friends.'

'There's always someone to help if you need it,' said Emily Hope. 'I'm doing the tombola.'

'And I'm in charge of the bottle stall,' said Ernie Bell.

'And I'm down for the book stall,' said Adam Hope.

Gran said gently, 'You really would be among friends.'

Miss Marjorie and Miss Joan looked at each other. 'I suppose we could,' said Miss Marjorie.

'It would be quite fun,' said Miss Joan, looking surprised at herself.

Mandy looked round the circle of faces, all intent on the Spry sisters. She didn't think it would be long before the sisters were part of village life. Not if Gran had her way.

Now was the moment. She and James could slip away quietly while the church bazaar was being discussed.

Carefully they carried the cages to the edge of the trees and carefully they set them down on the grass.

'I suppose we have to let them go,' said James. He was looking sad too.

Mandy nodded. 'Now?' she said. It was better to get it over with. She didn't think she could bear to drag it out.

'Now,' said James and together they lifted the latches on the cages.

For a moment nothing happened. Then the vixen sniffed the air delicately and stepped neatly out of her cage. Her coat gleamed in the sun and her ears stood straight and pricked for every sound. She turned this way and that, her eyes bright with health. She moved forward gracefully. She showed no sign of her injury now—not even the slightest limp.

Then Lucky pattered out of his cage and ran to her. Gently she nudged him

173

and he nuzzled her flank. Then she bent her head and gave him a push and made a low sound deep in her throat. He looked up at her and gave a sharp little bark in answer. Then all at once they were off, fast as the wind, heads up, tails flashing, running side by side through the trees, free as the air.

Mandy watched until they were no more than a blur through her tears. Then, at the edge of the densest part of the trees, the vixen stopped and turned. Lucky also stopped and looked back. Clear on the air came a high-pitched bark. Again and again it came.

Mandy felt the tears roll down her cheeks. She would miss Lucky so much. But she knew that a wild animal belonged in the wild. She wouldn't want Lucky caged, petted. She wanted him to be free—free as the wind that rustled the branches over her head. Free to roam and to wander and to live out his life the way nature intended him to. But it hurt to let him go.

Still the barking went on—until Mandy raised her hand and answered.

'Goodbye, Lucky,' she said as the two animals turned and were lost in the depths of the wood. 'Goodbye. Stay safe!'